WORTH OF WASTE

DELUCA DUET: PART TWO

BETHANY-KRIS

Published by Bethany-Kris

www.bethanykris.com

eISBN 13: 978-1-988197-27-2
Print ISBN 13: 978-1-988197-28-9

Cover Art © Jay Aheer
Editor: Nina S. Gooden

DEDICATION

To my littlest boy, Carson. You inspired JD/Junior and his antics.
You light up Mommy's life, sweet boy.

TABLE OF CONTENTS

CHAPTER 1

Karen

WHO are you?

Karen Martin woke up each and every day, asking herself that same question.

Who are you? How did you get here? Why did you do this to yourself?

She didn't have the right answers to tell her reflection in the mirror, certainly none that would explain her current situation, or the hell she had found herself living in. She also knew she had no one else to blame—mostly—other than her reflection staring back at her.

Maybe that was the worst part, the fact that she didn't have someone else to blame.

How could she, when she was alone?

Today was a harder day than normal, and those questions she always asked came with a little more force than normal, if only because the first thing she saw on the small television as she sat down with a cup of decaffeinated tea in her hands was *his* face.

The first thought that came to her mind?

That's a better picture than the mugshot.

A shot of Dino DeLuca sitting in the courtroom, suit and tie perfectly in place, standing as he handed his 'guilty' plea over. And then he was gone, the image fading away as the anchor room flashed back on the television where the anchors had already moved onto another story.

Karen had only caught the very tail end of the news story, but what she had seen was more than enough to know Dino wouldn't be coming back out anytime soon.

A sickness climbed from her sensitive stomach, and she set the tea aside, not daring to take another drink. She could have blamed it on the pregnancy—blamed her warring emotions on the little life just barely beginning—but it would have been an excuse.

She didn't know what to do.

She was alone.

She was pregnant.

She was scared.

An item caught her attention out of the corner of her eye, and for a second, those fears bled away and were then replaced by a heated anger swelling in her chest. The thick manila envelope, filled with stacks of cash and topped with a note Karen couldn't begin to understand, sat on the very edge of her coffee table.

She'd recognized Dino's handwriting on the package the second the mail man banged on her door and shoved it into her hands, pissed off because it was too big to put in her mailbox downstairs. She hadn't known what was happening to him at the time she'd gotten the package—that early Monday morning had just been another day for her, although a sadder, bleaker morning, given she had been convinced Dino's lack of presence was yet another sign that she would just have to move forward alone.

How stupid she had been …

How *crazy* …

Karen glared at the cash again, hating that she hadn't just taken it somewhere and handed it off to get it out of her hands. A charity, maybe.

The police, even.

She sighed.

No doubt, the police would be happy to get a package like that from Karen, especially if she could say it was from Dino. Something stopped her from doing either—the charity or the police.

Her pregnancy.

Dino's child.

The unborn life was the one and *only* thing that stopped Karen's anger from making her do something she might regret one day. She knew Dino hadn't meant any harm by sending her the money, and his note inside the package had only confirmed that fact, but the last few sentences of the scribbled mess had just left her more confused.

Don't give the child my names, it had read.

Karen tried not to dwell on that as much as she could, but it was becoming more and more impossible as the days went on. Especially on a day like today, when she happened to see something like the news broadcast on the television, yet she still felt so far removed from the entire scene.

Because she didn't *know*.

She didn't know anything about the legal problems, what Dino faced, when or *if* he might be out, or even how she could find out more without stepping foot into his business and making her presence known.

If nothing else, Karen had figured that one thing out all by herself and without any help.

Dino did *not* want Karen involved.

Not with his people.

Not with his life.

Not with the ... mafia.

It all felt a little surreal.

She met a man one day, a sad, frowning man who seemed so cold from afar, so entirely unapproachable on that foggy, damp morning. She'd watched him from nearby as he talked to a gravestone, his large hands being so very careful as they wiped off the stone with a pristine white napkin from his jacket pocket.

Karen had thought about how lonely he looked, crouched down in front of the grave. How alone he seemed, in his distant gaze that looked right passed her at one moment in time, not even noticing she was standing there by a tree watching him.

She should have known better, honestly.

She had no business interfering when she hadn't even known the man.

And yet, she did.

When Dino DeLuca smiled, Karen had felt like she won a battle that day.

She had done something *good*.

He made her feel amazing with nothing more than a grin.

In a way, Karen had put herself in her current position by not pressing harder for answers from Dino over the course of their year-and-a-half-long relationship. Times when he flaked on her without explanation, other moments when he seemed quieter than normal—though he barely talked as it was—and passing comments from others about his side business and other life that she allowed to fly right over head.

Maybe she pretended like he was exactly what he seemed because she didn't want to know about the rest.

Or maybe she didn't ask things she should have because she wouldn't have liked the answers.

Karen prided herself on the fact that she wasn't stupid. For the most part, she made rational, educated choices about her life and the people in it. She didn't like negativity, but rather, filled her days with goodness and happiness to keep all the darkness at bay.

Then there was Dino ...

A man who seemed almost swathed in an aura of darkness he couldn't—or didn't want to—escape from.

She hadn't minded that. He drew her in like a moth to the brightly-burning flame, and while his actions promised never to burn her, his soul never said a damn thing.

Who was really at fault here?

Certainly not him.

The news program ended, switching over to an early morning panel sitting around a glass table with hosts ready to gossip about the latest in politics, fashion, and the celebrity life. Karen wasn't really seeing what was on the show, but rather, the image of Dino standing in the courtroom.

It had burned into her brain.

She couldn't get the image out.

Who are you?

That was all she wanted to ask him.

She just wanted one more minute of his time—a few passing seconds—to ask the one question she should have demanded he answer over and over again.

What would he even say now?

I'm a criminal.

I don't live a good life.

I lied to you.

I love you.

Pushing those awful fucking thoughts from her mind, Karen grabbed the remote and shut the television off, hoping it would rid the image from her mind. It didn't; she should have known better than to try.

Like that first time they'd met, this was no different.

Dino's black soul had imprinted itself inside Karen's heart without even trying. He should have warned her, maybe, given her a chance to run when she could have, before she got too mixed up in him.

Deep down, she didn't want that at all.

And in a way, he *had* given her that chance.

Tell me to leave and I'll go, he'd told her again and again.

She hadn't ever told him those words because she hadn't wanted to. Not when she knew something was wrong with him, not when she knew he was hiding things from her, and not even when he'd hurt her by walking away when she needed him to stay.

Karen didn't say things she didn't mean, after all.

That didn't mean it was easy, or that she understood where all of this was going to lead her in the end. She had the distinct feeling nothing would make sense or feel particularly good until she had the chance to sit down with Dino once and for all to get the answers she craved, to questions he had refused to entertain over and over again.

But she would get those answers … eventually.

Karen had long since decided on that.

She just had to figure out *how*.

Well, actually, Dino would have to wait a short while longer. She had something more important to deal with, or rather, figure out what in the hell she was going to do about and how she was going to make it work.

Her baby, that was.

As much as she wanted to go and demand answers from Dino, as deep as her need was to simply talk to him and hug him, even if she *was* angry with him, she had something else to take care of and she didn't think he would mind.

That was never more apparent to Karen than when she flew off the couch and headed for the bathroom faster than she thought was possible, her hand thrown over her mouth in a shitty attempt to keep the spilling vomit inside for those last few feet.

Thankfully, she made it in time. That didn't necessarily make vomiting any more fun.

Morning sickness was a bitch.

The books all said the sickness would probably wane by the

second trimester, but Karen still had weeks and weeks to go for that just yet. Her stress and worries weren't helping her sensitive stomach in the least, considering the worse she felt mentally or physically, the sicker she became.

It was almost like her morning sickness was reflecting her moods, if that were possible.

It wasn't just Dino she was worried about, either.

It was also herself.

She lived in a too-small apartment with only one bedroom. The place didn't have nearly enough room for all the things a baby needed. Not that she had the money to actually go out and buy the things the baby would need, because she didn't have any money at all. All the savings she had managed to accumulate over the years was a dwindling pile of cash—now that she had quit her job at Dino's restaurant—and she needed to fund herself and keep herself housed and fed until another job popped up.

But who was going to give a job to a woman with a taste for photography, bookkeeping skills, and a baby on the way?

Her situation was looking bleaker every single day.

You could go home, her mind pressed.

Karen didn't even want to entertain the idea of returning to California where her parents lived, if only because the shame would eat her alive. Not only would she be forced to admit to her parents that Chicago had turned out to be a massive failure on her part, she would also be left explaining her pregnancy and just how all that came about.

She was an adult, for Christ's sake.

She could and would figure this out on her own.

Somehow.

After finishing in the bathroom and putting the mouthwash to good use for the third time that morning, Karen went back to her tea in the living room, though she didn't bother to drink it. Instead, she took it to the kitchen and dumped the contents out, as her thirst and appetite was entirely gone.

Leaning back against the cupboards, she massaged her temples with the pads of her fingers, hoping to relieve some of the tension there.

It didn't help all that much.

From the other side of the apartment, the manila envelope with its cash spilling out caught her attention again.

Goddammit.

She had resolved herself *not* to entertain the idea.

Not to touch the money.

Life probably wasn't going to give her much of a choice.

The baby *was* the most important thing, Karen knew.

First, though, she had to talk to Dino.

Those last few words on the note haunted her for reasons she wasn't willing to face.

She needed to know *why.*

He was the only one who could tell her.

CHAPTER 2

Dino

A LOUD clanging from outside the cell woke the man in the bunk under Dino DeLuca's bed. Probably a prisoner from one of the neighboring cells, attempting to annoy the guards and start an issue.

When the inmates got bored, things like this happened.

He listened to his cellmate curse a blue streak, roll off the bed onto the hard cement floor, and then slowly came to the realization of where he was again. The young man—his cellmate, Todd—was only twenty-three years old and looking at ten to fifteen years for a sentence on drug trafficking. The guy's almost-boyish appearance, with his blue eyes and blond hair that stuck up in every direction, made the charges hard to believe. Todd was lucky if he weighed one-fifty, soaking wet, and he spoke quietly, rarely looking anyone in the eye when he did talk to them.

But here the kid was, with a Mafioso for a cellmate, with a heavy sentence and drug charges on his record.

Todd didn't talk to Dino about how or why he'd found himself in the prison beyond the information on the charges and sentence he faced, and Dino didn't ask for more than the kid gave. However, each morning the kid woke up, it was as though he was only realizing in that moment that he wasn't waking up in his own bed, but rather, a small eight-by-eight, cement room with one wall of bars, and a *very* small window that was too high to see out of— and too small to climb out of it, should one of them actually reach it.

It happened every day with no sign of changing.

"Careful, Todd," Dino said, his attention focused on the crossword in his hands.

Todd took a heavy gulp of air, sitting up on the floor as his gaze focused in on Dino for the first time that morning.

Strangely, Dino often found himself grateful that he'd ended up with a cellmate like Todd. He could have ended up with a bastard, or worse … Instead, he got a kid that almost reminded him of his younger brother. That was, if Theo DeLuca were stripped of his demeanor and behavior.

So, maybe not entirely like his brother, but Dino looked out for Todd, when he could, outside of their cell. He was too small, too young, and the other inmates—or some—would not think twice about using Todd's weaknesses to their advantage for whatever fucking horrible thing they wanted.

"Sleep last night?" Todd asked.

Dino almost smiled, but the amusement quickly faded. "An hour or so."

That was what he always told his cellmate, whether he did or did not get any sleep. Todd rarely asked about Dino's odd sleeping habits, but he figured that was because the kid didn't want Dino calling him out on the way *he* woke up every morning.

Tit for tat, he supposed.

Todd stood from the floor, tossing the sheet back to his two-inch thick mattress. "Visiting day today, right?"

Dino shrugged.

How should he know?

He didn't get visitors unless it was his lawyer, and a visit from Mike was rare unless Dino had specifically called the guy in.

"We've been cellmates for thirty-two days," Todd noted.

"Do you have a calendar that you're keeping track of or something?" Dino asked.

"I remember numbers."

Interesting.

Dino wasn't sure what Todd's penchant for tracking days had to do with him. "What about it, kid?"

"I noticed you don't talk much."

"I noticed you don't look people in the face when you talk to them."

15

Todd glanced up at Dino on the top bunk, then quickly looked away. "Point taken."

Exactly.

Dino looked over his crossword again, trying to pass time before their block would be called out for breakfast. He couldn't get beyond the hint. Todd wasn't only good with numbers, he had learned.

"Cat—five letter word, starts with an 'M' and ends with a 'Y.'"

Todd didn't even glance back as he brushed his teeth at the small metal sink, "Uh, a moggy."

What the fuck was a moggy?

How did this kid even end up in prison?

"You're too smart for this place," Dino muttered, more to himself than his cellmate.

All over again, Dino was reminded of his younger brother Theo, and how much he wanted to keep him from ending up in a situation like this. Dino had found himself in lockup because of his asshole uncle and Ben DeLuca's meddling. He didn't want Theo to end up the same way.

Or God, someone else close to Dino …

He shook his head, refusing to even let his thoughts go there.

He'd done okay since pleading guilty a month ago and having his sentence handed over on the drug and weapons charges. He'd stuck to the schedule the prison put him on because it helped to make the hours pass by easier. He didn't cause shit, because he was hoping for reduced time, and kicking someone's head in would only earn him more months behind bars, plus solitary confinement.

He certainly hadn't thought of *her.*

Not at night when his cellmate slept.

Not during the one hour a day when he got to go outside and breathe real air.

Not when he wasted time working on stupid fucking crossword puzzles.

Karen.

The moment her name passed through his mind in a whisper, Dino felt an aching emptiness start to grow in his chest.

This was why he tried not to think of her, why he couldn't do it.

She would be better off without him, he knew. She could start over, if that's what was best for her, and shit, maybe she'd get the hell out of Chicago and go as far away as she could possibly get with the money he'd sent to her before his arrest had happened. She could raise his child away from the danger that he and his life posed to them.

If she were a smart woman, those were the exact things she whould do.

Dino wouldn't blame her at all.

No, Dino tried not to think of Karen Martin at all.

Except he did.

Every damn day.

All the fucking time.

He loved her, after all.

He hoped she had done none of those things. He hoped she had figured out a way to stay, that she had used his money, and maybe—God, maybe—she'd be waiting for that explanation he had promised all those months ago.

Still …

Dino had to pretend like he didn't want any of those things.

It was easier to remember why he had gotten where he was and what he was going to do when he was out, if he didn't focus on only her. Someday, he'd be able to do that for Karen and give her what she deserved to have from him.

Someday.

Today was just not that day.

"Visiting day, you said?" Dino asked, tossing his crossword puzzle and pencil aside before he jumped down from the top bunk. "Do you have someone coming to visit you today, or what?"

Todd was already at the bars, his arms hanging out between the holes as he looked for one of the guards that would signal breakfast was soon. "Maybe."

"Maybe is a non-answer, kid."

"Maybe I wait every week, thinking this will be the one she actually shows up to, but she never comes."

Dino's brow rose high. "*She?*"

Shit, he actually thought Todd might have been gay. Not that he would have cared if the kid was, but it was surprising that he had a *she* in his life that he talked about with a sort of fondness that did not speak of a family relation. After all, Dino had heard the kid talk about his mother and sister, and he didn't use that kind of tone.

"Yeah, she," Todd repeated. "She—the one that I ended up in here for."

Well, then …

Dino wasn't touching that.

Tit for tat, you know.

"Good luck with that," Dino muttered.

Todd didn't reply.

The guards shouted out for the block as the buzzers started above the cell doors, and the bars slid open.

Breakfast was served.

Not that it would be anything good.

Because Dino's block in the prison happened to house non-violent offenders as the general population, they were lucky enough to have their cells open for a majority of the afternoon. The inmates were allowed to wander around the block and as long as no trouble was started, the guards wouldn't hit the alarm and push the button to lock all the cell doors.

Dino had only had one problem during the free-cell time.

Once, he'd been on the lower level where the cafeteria was located, sitting in the corner and looking out the barred Plexiglas windows. Something had prickled at the back of his neck—a sensation he hadn't felt in a long time.

Like his long-dormant instincts were suddenly waking back up.

He'd found Todd in their cell, beaten bloody, and some of their things missing. It hadn't taken long to figure out *who* had done it, once Todd had woken up. Dino had gotten the bastard back on the next free-cell time, when the guards' backs were turned and the inmate's cellmate had gone downstairs, just like Dino had the day before.

Prison liked its tit for tat.

Dino simply provided that without getting himself in shit.

Thankfully, there hadn't been an issue since, and guards were more than willing to turn their cheek to a bruise or bloody nose when inmates worked out their own problems without a fucking riot of some sort. He had also effectively sealed his reputation amongst the prisoners that he wasn't going to take shit from anybody, and that included someone bothering his cellmate.

"DeLuca!"

Dino damn near fell off the top bunk at the shout of his name. He'd been lost in his zone, enjoying the quiet that the block was rarely afforded. It was one of the only things he really enjoyed about visitation days. Most of the inmates on his block had someone who showed up, and they'd either be put into the visitation area, or be placed in the waiting area for when their time came.

Todd had gotten his visitor, as far as Dino knew.

He'd been called down to the waiting area earlier, leaving Dino alone to his thoughts. He didn't mind.

As the guard came into view outside of Dino's cell, the blue-suited man tapped his knuckles against the door, glancing up at the camera. "Open it for me."

"What is it?" Dino asked.

The guard didn't answer, simply waited for his request to be heeded. It was only *after* the door was unlocked and the bars slid open did he turn his attention back to Dino. "You've got a visitor downstairs. Apparently, they didn't register that they were coming in, so they had to wait for when there was a cancelation in the schedule."

What?

Dino pushed off the bed, landing soundlessly on the cement floor. "Who is it?"

"I don't get details, DeLuca, just orders."

As the guard cuffed Dino—common procedure when inmates were being moved between blocks where it was less secure than other areas of the prison—he considered who might have shown up.

His uncle was a good possibility.

Ben DeLuca hadn't come to the prison once since Dino's arrival, but he figured he was due one of his uncle's usual threats that would remind him of just how and why he was there in the first fucking place.

His brother was another option.

Theo had come to the first hearing with a clean suit for Dino to wear. Even though Dino would never ask for his brother to show up like he had. That would only put Theo on Ben's shit list.

Being a Capo for the Chicago Outfit, meant Dino wasn't likely to have a lot of visitors by way of friends or family. No man affiliated to the mob wanted to be seen having interactions with another man who was locked up. It simply wouldn't look good, and it didn't lend any credence to a man's reputation of staying away from cops or officials. It would be better for any sort of interaction from a man outside and a man inside to be had over a phone call, and even then, very little talk of business or the mafia was likely to be had.

It was an unspoken rule of the lifestyle.

Women were the only exception to the rule, but his mother was long dead, and his sister was out of the country.

Dino shouldn't have a visitor.

He hadn't called his lawyer in.

He didn't have family or friends that were unconnected to the mob.

Who in the hell was it?

"Let's go," the guard said, directing Dino out of the cell.

He would find out soon enough.

CHAPTER 3

Karen

KAREN hadn't thought about how cold a prison must feel like on the inside. She had always been the passerby on the outside, getting just a glimpse of the large building with its concrete walls. She hadn't actually given much thought as to how the people inside must feel to be locked away.

Of course, she knew criminals deserved to be exactly where they were—locked up, hidden away from society to do their time.

She was not naive to what prisons were meant for, she simply hadn't been put in a position where she needed to *care* about the people—or rather, one person—inside the concrete walls. Until now, it seemed.

Karen tugged her jacket closer to her chest, trying not to be bothered by the guards on both sides of the Plexiglas windows. The hard chair was doing nothing to soothe the sudden ache in her back, and even sitting didn't help the restlessness coursing through her nervous system.

She still wasn't sure if she should have come to visit Dino. A part of her wanted to see him, needed to talk to him, if only for a few minutes. She needed answers that only he could give her, but whether or not he would be willing to talk was a whole other story.

The other part of her, a little louder than the part that wanted to be where she was, had her squirming in her seat with an anxious flare that just wouldn't let go, no matter how hard she tried to ignore it.

Maybe she shouldn't have come at all.

Shit, as it were, it had taken her a good two weeks just to gain up the courage to go looking for where Dino had been placed, and then another two weeks to talk herself into a visit. Karen hadn't realized just how involved visiting an inmate actually was. There was much more to it than just showing up and asking for time to see a prisoner.

She had been smart enough to call ahead and find out if there were scheduled visiting days, but no one had thought to mention during that phone call that visitors needed to sign in, reserve certain times, plus go through a *massive* amount of security before they could even get their visit with an inmate.

Showing up with no previous sign-in, no visiting reservation, and having no clue how the security for the prison was actually run, Karen had been left waiting for hours on the off chance that someone might flake on their visiting time.

She hadn't even been guaranteed a visit with Dino when she finally got through the sign-in information, but rather, shoved into a waiting area where she fiddled with her phone and stared at gray walls for hours.

Thankfully, someone hadn't shown up for their visitation, and Karen was walked through another hallway and sat down in a hard chair, facing a Plexiglas window where she could see another chair waited. On the walls of both sides of the glass, phones sat waiting for her to pick up one, and Dino to pick up the other. Thin barrier walls separated her seating section from a row of several others.

The barriers did nothing to help hide the conversations going on.

She could still hear the conversations of others visiting inmates, though she couldn't hear what the inmates were saying from their side of the wall, or even see them behind their barriers.

Hearing them was more than enough.

A mother talking to her son.

A girlfriend crying to her boyfriend.

A friend reassuring his friend.

Karen wished there was a bit more privacy offered for people, but as soon as the thought came on, she knew how ridiculous it was. This was prison, for fuck's sake.

There was no privacy.

No one expected any sort of discretion.

That was probably her first real understanding that coming to the prison to see and talk to Dino was absolutely a mistake. It didn't matter that a huge portion of her heart was still owned by a man she didn't really know at all. It didn't make a difference that his lies did little to cut away at the feelings she still held for him.

The questions she wanted to ask—the things she needed to know—could not be asked *here*.

Still, even knowing this, Karen didn't move from her chair. Her fingers drummed a fast beat to the small ledge that acted as a shelf in front of the Plexiglas window.

Just knowing she would *see* Dino was enough to make her stay there.

Tiny, smudged finger and palm prints on the edge of the glass caught her attention, and she could tell immediately that by the size of the prints, they were owned by someone small. A child, probably. It looked as though they had put their whole little hands against the glass, almost as if they thought if they could push hard enough on the window, if they got a little bit closer, then they would be able to crawl right through it.

For a split second, caught by the sight of those smudged prints, Karen was ... *heartbroken.*

Would that be her child someday?

Would it be her baby learning who its father was and finding love on the other side of a Plexiglas window?

Would it be her son or daughter's fingerprints breaking someone else's heart at the heavy realization of what sitting in that spot meant for their future?

Karen blinked away the sudden prickling sensation in her eyes, willing the wetness gathering to go away. She couldn't afford a breakdown. Not now, not here. When she was alone, when there weren't guards just down the way and cameras trained on her every move, then maybe she could take a moment to let her situation sink in and deal with how all of this made her feel, and what it would mean.

She had only glanced over her shoulder to check the time on the clock behind her for a second before a knock on the glass made her spin back around in her seat.

A guard was standing on the other side of the glass, his hand still lifted with his knuckles coming forward to hit the window again if he needed.

Karen wasn't paying attention to him at all.

No, she was too busy staring at the man *behind* him.

Dino met Karen's gaze as the guard said something she couldn't hear, and then turned to leave without another word. The man she had thought about for weeks on end, the man she worried and fretted over, the man she had been so angry with and hurt by his actions, only stared at her, never moving or even attempting to sit and grab the phone at the wall.

No, he just fucking *stared at her.* Karen sucked in a hard breath, a deep pain settling in the middle of her chest. She hadn't thought about how hard it would be to see him locked up, locked down, and out of her reach.

The gray uniform and cuffs around his wrists only added to that difficult, painful emptiness growing in her soul.

Those words she had wanted to ask, all the things she wanted to say, suddenly stuck on her tongue like cement.

They wouldn't come.

The words wouldn't form.

Even when Karen reached for the phone, putting it to her ear and looking to Dino expectantly, he didn't move. He didn't sit or reach for his own phone, but rather, kept staring at her as though he wasn't sure *what* he was seeing.

"Talk to me?" Karen asked, hoping he understood what she was saying without needing to hear it.

Then, all at once, it was like Dino had woken up from his daze. He still didn't pick up the phone, but he shook his head quickly and mouthed, "You shouldn't be here, Karen."

All over again, her heart broke.

"But—"

She was going to tell him she missed him—*loved* him.

She wanted to tell him about the baby, how far along the pregnancy was, and when she was due.

She needed to ask what in the hell she was supposed to do?

Dino didn't give her a chance to ask or say anything. "Go home."

Karen blinked, sitting a little straighter in her chair. "What?"

He pointed at her, then behind her. "Go home and don't come back here."

She didn't move, because something inside wouldn't let her go. His rejection stung like acid on her skin, but the coldness reflecting in his brown gaze was something far worse, as far as she was concerned. She had broken through that coldness once, a long time ago. She had been able to see the small bit of light that colored the edges of his blackened soul.

There was so much more to Dino DeLuca than what he showed.

No one truly knew.

Except for maybe her.

Dino dropped Karen's gaze when she still stayed right where she was, not budging even an inch. Then, he reached over and grabbed the phone, putting it to his ear. For a long moment, Karen cradled her own phone tighter, listening to the rhythmic crackle of Dino's breaths through the speaker.

"I'm sorry," he whispered.

That was not what she expected to hear.

She didn't ask him what he was apologizing for because without needing to tell her, they both knew damn well he had a lot to offer her where repentance was concerned. He had done a lot of things, said a lot of things, and it had left them with nothing more than Plexiglas windows and two phones away from one another.

"You have to go," Dino said, still keeping that soft tone, "because it's not safe for you to be here."

Karen shook her head. "You'd be surprised at just how safe this place is for housing thousands of criminals."

Dino flinched. "Not the people here—the people who are outside of here."

She suspected he meant his family, that other life that he'd kept hidden from her until she didn't have a choice but to open her eyes and see *everything* Dino had been hiding.

"Dino—"

His gaze met hers, dark and sure.

There was fear there, and she hadn't expected to see that at all.

The last thing she had ever seen from Dino was *fear.*

"It's not safe for you to be coming here," he repeated firmly.

With that, he put the phone back to the hook, and turned away. He'd only taken one step, probably moving toward a waiting guard that she couldn't see, before Karen was up off the chair and moving closer to the window.

Her hands slammed into the Plexiglas window hard, making Dino stop. She'd dropped the phone to the small ledge, not even bothering to hang it up like he had for his. Those tears she had been holding at bay started to fall, making tracks down her cheeks as she stared at the man who refused to even talk to her.

"Dino!"

Her shout of his name must have been loud enough for him to hear behind the glass, because his back tensed. He looked over his shoulder at her, that fear still present, but it was accompanied by something else, too.

Understanding, maybe?

A bit of want, too.

She had so many things to say to him, so many things to ask.

Those same questions she had been asking herself for a good month and a half fought their way out, demanding to be spoken aloud so that maybe ... God, maybe, she would *finally* be able to sleep at night.

"I don't *know* who you are," Karen told him, hoping he could read her lips enough to understand what she had said.

She loved the man she thought she knew.

She cared for the person who let her chase his nightmares away.

She wanted to hold the man who made her feel like she was the most important thing in his world.

But the man standing behind the glass, the one with a last name that she now knew should frighten her, and affiliations that labeled him one of the worst kinds of criminals ...

No, Karen didn't know that man at all.

But she wanted to.

Because she believed, no matter what, she'd love him, too.

"I'm sorry," Dino mouthed. "I'll see you soon."

That was it.

That was all he said.

Dino was gone before Karen could even think about what she wanted to do or say next. All she saw was his back as he disappeared beyond the barrier, and he didn't even look back at her that time.

She fell into the hard chair with a thump, suddenly feeling so unsteady and unsure.

Had she made a mistake?

Was she wrong for wanting that man?

I'll see you soon.

His words rang through her mind like a clanging bell, over and over again. It left her feeling more unsure than ever, like her world had suddenly been put on pause because he wasn't kind enough to tell her this was the end.

Instead, he'd put them on *hold*.

Dino didn't seem to understand that it couldn't work that way for Karen. While he was locked away and unable to explain himself to her, the world wouldn't stop for her while she waited for him to get out.

Her world still turned.

She was still pregnant.

She had to keep moving forward so that she could do what she needed to do in order to care for his child. She wouldn't keep putting herself through hell emotionally, on the off chance that Dino might give something more to her than a look that made her heart clench and words that only cut her deeper.

She wouldn't be coming back to the prison at all after today. She had given him the chance to tell her who he was and what he needed or wanted from her, and he hadn't even tried to provide her with those things.

Dino cared.

He loved her.

Karen knew those things without a doubt.

The problem was, love couldn't always be enough and no matter what people tried to say, it couldn't be unconditional. Love without barriers meant no one thought about the other side of the equation—they didn't take into account how their behavior or actions might hurt someone else.

It was selfish to love that way.

It was unhealthy.

Yet, a small part of her still didn't care.

I'll see you soon.

Maybe by the time he was ready—by the time he *could* give her what she needed—Karen wouldn't need or want it anymore. The part of her that he owned could be put on the shelf for a time while she waited on him, but the rest of her was still going to have to keep moving.

She was worried the rest of her would eventually take the waiting part with it, too.

That probably scared her the most.

CHAPTER 4

Karen

IT had taken Karen a long time—long enough that a guard had come to tell her she needed to leave so the next visitor could come in—for her to stand up and ready to leave the prison. The heaviness in her heart wouldn't leave, no matter what she did.

It was a long drive home from the prison to her apartment in upper Chicago, and she wasn't exactly looking forward to the silence. When she was alone, her second thoughts and misdeeds were far more apparent, and since she didn't have anyone else to talk to, she was left with talking to her damn self.

There had been a time once when Karen didn't mind talking to herself; she hadn't minded her own company.

Those days were long gone.

On the drive home, Karen turned the radio up loud enough to drown out her own thoughts. She certainly hurt, but she wasn't going to add to the pile with her own guilty conscience.

Thankfully, the drive home went by far quicker than she thought it would. It was only when her apartment building was in sight did she start to feel slightly normal again, a calm sense of relief sweeping over her senses.

Strange, how that worked …

A person didn't know how much they should appreciate freedom until they were forced to see what it was like for those who had their freedom taken away.

Karen shook her head to rid those thoughts, parking the car in her allotted spot and making her way to the building entrance. She unlocked the entrance door, ignoring the slight tremor rocking her hand from the emotions still building up steam in her body. She'd done well to pretend on the drive home that her life wasn't falling apart.

Now that she was almost home, those traitorous emotions were beginning to spill over.

She barely noticed her neighbor balancing two brown bags of groceries just across from her own apartment as she fumbled with the lock.

Just a couple more seconds, and she could … do whatever she needed to do.

Cry.

Break down.

Wallow for a while.

"Oh, Karen!"

Apparently, she wasn't the only one with attention that was elsewhere. Her neighbor only noticed she was unlocking her apartment as she pushed the door open.

Karen cursed inside her head, wishing the older woman hadn't stopped her, if only because she wanted to get the hell inside her apartment and hide away from the rest of the world for a while. She couldn't exactly be rude to an old woman—it wasn't Karen's style.

Bess was in her late fifties, and lived alone. She rarely had guests, except for the occasional yearly visit from her daughter who had moved to Colorado years ago. She did well for being older and living on her own, barely asking for help and only if something was very important. However, she did invite Karen over for dinner or tea occasionally.

Karen never said no.

She didn't want today to be the first day when she had to refuse Bess.

Clearing her throat and hoping the emotion was gone from her tone, Karen turned slightly and asked, "Yes?"

"Here, take these a moment." Bess pushed both bags of groceries into Karen's arms, shooting the younger woman a warm, but apologetic smile at the same time. "Damn key keeps sticking."

"You should talk to the building manager about that, Bess."

"I am—I will. He's a tad useless, though, isn't he?"

Karen found herself smiling at Bess's mutterings. The older woman fumbled with her key and the deadbolt for another ten seconds before she finally got the lock to unlatch. Bess pushed open her door and turned to take the groceries from Karen with another sheepish smile.

"Thank you, dear."

Karen shrugged. "No problem. I'm just going to—"

"Well, wait a moment," Bess interrupted, "so I don't forget again."

Forget what?

Karen was too tired to voice her confusion, but since Bess didn't invite her inside when the old woman disappeared into her apartment, she figured it didn't matter. If Bess had wanted her to come over for dinner or tea, she would already be in the lady's apartment.

That was just how Bess worked.

She didn't take "No" for an answer.

Karen waited another minute or two before Bess finally reappeared in her doorway, a white envelope in her hands. The scrawl across the front was not familiar, but her name and address was still perfectly written in block letters.

"The mail man must have shoved it into my box by accident," Bess said, handing the envelope over to Karen.

For a long while, Karen stared at the envelope, not moving or even speaking to thank Bess for the mail. Maybe it was the largely written DO NOT RETURN TO SENDER in the top left-hand corner that made Karen pause. The money Dino had sent to her months ago had arrived with the same message in the return address spot.

Had he sent her something else?

The handwriting was not the same as Dino's, of that Karen was sure, but that didn't stop her from wondering.

"It came about two and a half weeks ago," Bess said, "but I kept forgetting to bring it to you."

Karen waved off Bess's concerns. "It's fine."

Why was her voice so faint?

Bess took note of Karen's sudden change in demeanor, asking, "Are you okay, dear? I couldn't help but notice I haven't been seeing a lot of you, coming and going like you usually do around the building lately. Probably one of the reasons why I kept forgetting I had your mail."

Only an elderly person could be nosy and not be rude about it at the same time.

Karen appreciated Bess's concern, but she didn't want to weigh her old neighbor down with details of her life she wasn't even sure she was supposed to share. Never mind the fact she just wasn't in the mood to talk lately.

"I'm fine," Karen said, flashing Bess a smile she hoped was enough to ward off any further worries the woman might have. "Thank you for this."

She waved the envelope high, and Bess nodded in response.

"I'm just across the hall if you need anything, dear," Bess said.

"And the same goes for you."

One quick hug that Bess had given with no questions asked later, and the old woman was gone, disappearing back into her apartment and shutting the door. Karen was left alone in the hall, and it took her far longer than she wanted to admit before she realized she was free to hide away in her own apartment like she had wanted to all damn day.

Closing her apartment door, latching the deadbolt, and taking off her boots and jacket had never felt better. Karen tried not to dwell on the odd envelope sitting on her kitchen table as she readied a cup of ginger tea. She was less likely to have a spell of morning sickness after she ate dinner, if she drank the tea while she ate.

Also, morning sickness was a complete and total myth.

That curse came and went whenever it felt like it.

Given she was well into her second trimester of pregnancy, it should have started to wane a bit. Maybe it had a little, considering instead of every day—sometimes twice a day—she only experienced it a couple times a week now.

That was something to be grateful for, right?

The small business card reminder on her fridge caught her attention as she opened the door to pull out leftovers from the night before to reheat.

21 week ultrasound appointment, it read.

Karen stared at the date scrawled in the timeslot, realizing how soon that was approaching. She would find out the gender of the baby, and be reassured everything was looking normal as far as development went. And she would finally be able to *see* her baby.

She'd had an ultrasound early in the pregnancy, due to the fact she was approaching thirty years of age and this was her first pregnancy. Although the ultrasound had gone quite well, and the tech praised the baby and pointed it out on the screen for her to see, all Karen could distinguish was a tiny peanut-shaped blob.

A blob that was sucking the energy out of her, giving her emotional whiplash, *and* making her sick on a regular basis.

Then again, at that point, she really hadn't connected to the fact she was pregnant. That, or she hadn't been ready to at that time.

The bigger problem was the fact that Karen didn't have a whole lot of money to be throwing away on doctor's appointments because healthcare was fucking expensive and she didn't have a damn *job*. Her savings were already gone, but her rent was paid for another two months.

You do have money, her mind reminded her, *right under your bed in a shoebox*.

Karen still hadn't conceded to the idea of using Dino's money for her needs. She didn't know where the money had come from, or if it was a byproduct of his business. It probably was. She wasn't sure if she was okay with that.

Doesn't matter. Baby comes first. Deal with it later.

Karen sighed, knowing her inner voice was right.

Whether she liked it or not, Dino *had* provided her with a way to care for herself and their child, at least until she got back on her feet and could handle her business again.

That didn't mean she particularly had to like it.

Once Karen had the leftovers heating in the microwave, she sat down at the table and reached for the envelope again. She fingered the edges of the white paper, wondering once more if this had somehow come from Dino.

It was only *after* she had it opened, pulled out the few papers, and unfolded them, did she know for sure it had come from him … somehow. While the handwriting on the outside hadn't been Dino's, the content on the inside was absolutely his.

Karen wasn't sure how long she sat there staring at the letters and words that didn't seem to make sense. And it wasn't because the letter itself didn't make sense, but because the ink of the pen that Dino had used to write seemed to bleed together right before her eyes.

Finally, those tears she had been holding back fell.

Four entire minutes passed before Karen was able to clear away the tears enough to actually *read* the letter in her hands. In just the first few sentences, she understood clearly how Dino had been able to get the letter to her with no stamp attached that said it had come from a jailhouse or a prison. His lawyer would be sending it for him, he had explained, and he had written it shortly before he agreed to the deal the prosecution had offered him.

The date in the top right-hand corner confirmed what he had written down below.

Bess might have only gotten the letter two and a half weeks earlier, but Dino had written it over a month ago. Karen reached for the envelope, noting the time stamp printed across the front. The letter had been sent a good week *after* Dino had written it.

Karen couldn't help but wonder if *this* was what she had been looking for?

Was this the answers to the questions keeping her up at night?

Would she finally be able to understand just who Dino DeLuca was and why he had done what he did?

Karen kept reading, and by the time she was halfway down the first page, the tears started to well again and her chest got terribly tight with an ache she hadn't felt in a long time.

I'm sorry I lied to you by hiding things from you; I knew—I thought I knew—that you wouldn't want me as I was, but instead, who you thought I was, he had written, his handwriting becoming messier in the spots where his feelings became clearer and his tone was less clinical. *I've never had to be just myself with someone, because my whole life has been wrapped up in a neat little bow to be everything that everyone else wanted.*

Karen almost wanted to stop reading—it would have been easier.

She probably could have held onto her anger and bitterness for a little while longer.

She wouldn't have had to feel guilty about walking away from someone she didn't know who had hurt her so badly.

Except reading Dino's words ... she found she did know him.

Or the parts that mattered.

An orphaned boy, left to look after his siblings. Abusive guardians.

He felt like the sacrifice, she thought, as she took in his explanation of why he didn't mind taking the abuse so his siblings wouldn't have to deal with it, or at least, not as badly as he did.

As Karen read Dino's words, from the first page to that very final fifth one, she realized she knew exactly who this man was. She wasn't entirely sure why she had thought that she didn't know him, because he had already given her a lot of these words in bits and pieces, in his actions and behaviors, and in the things he *wouldn't* do during their time together.

Never had she understood how truly worthless Dino felt about himself than she did as she read his words over and over again.

He saw himself as disposable.

He didn't want to be loved because he didn't deserve to be.

He might not have written those exact words, but they still rang out loudly and repeatedly.

At the very end, he had answered something that bothered her so much for so long. Ever since that packet of money had arrived on her doorstep with nothing more than a hastily scrawled note that explained the cash away.

Except it also stung with its final words, too.

Do not give the child my names.

She would never be able to forget that.

But in this letter, she saw his reasoning and heard his request without the pain stabbing into her heart at the same time.

I want better for my child, Karen. I don't know how to be a father or if I can even be one, but I know they deserve better. Something more than a last name that will forever be tied to something that will label him or her as a bad seed. Something else, other than a family name that reminds me of pain and secrets hidden behind closed doors. I want my child to be safe, to be free. I've never been free.

Karen dropped the papers to the table, but her gaze found his last few words.

The closest I ever came to freedom was you.

I love you. I'm sorry, even if you don't know what for.

I'll see you soon. —Dino

CHAPTER
5

Dino

COUNTING down days was no longer working as a way to pass time for Dino. It was not enough for him to know he had already served six months of his sentence, with another year to go. If anything, counting the days had only made it feel like slowing time down.

What was the old saying?

A watched pot never boiled.

Instead, he'd started counting the blobs of stucco on the ceiling of his cell, making almost a game out of how high of a number he could reach before something—or someone—would interrupt him.

251, 252, 253 ...

Thankfully, his cellmate was a quiet individual, for the most part, who had learned to sleep eighteen hours out of the day. Dino wasn't much of a fucking conversationalist anyway, and he didn't offer much beyond the good morning quip. He looked out for his cellmate, though, which was as much as he could give.

Or wanted to, for that matter.

265, 266, 267 ...

As he drifted into his focus of counting the small gray blobs above his head, Dino was able to drown out the sounds of the cell block outside of his cell. He could push away the chattering of the inmates and the shouts of the guards when the men got too loud.

But most of all—*best* of all—he was able to block out his own thoughts.

It seemed like when he was the quietest, his thoughts betrayed him the worst.

Especially now that he had far, *far* too much time to do nothing but lie on his back and think about everything and anything that came to his mind. Dino hadn't been much of an overthinker before prison, but being locked in a small room for the majority of his day with nothing but his regrets and thoughts to keep him company, he found he was quite capable of overthinking just about anything that flew into his mind.

He wished he didn't have to think at all.

Actually, he wished he was more like his cellmate, Todd. Capable of shutting his body down for the majority of the day, disappearing into a dreamless state and away from the hell they were currently stuck in.

Now that … *that* was a dream.

Dino wasn't that lucky, it seemed.

298, 299, 30—

"DeLuca, get your ass up, your lawyer is waiting on you!"

Dino's gaze drifted from the stucco on the ceiling to the guard waiting on the other side of the bars keeping him locked away. He was both irritated and slightly amused at being interrupted in his little game. He had been just ten blobs off from beating his record.

He didn't make an effort to move as fast as the guard wanted him to, not even when the guy tapped his stick against the metal, making it clang loud enough to wake Todd in the bunk below.

"What the fuck?" Todd grumbled, damn near falling out of the bed.

"Nothing," Dino muttered, pushing off the top bunk. His laceless sneakers hit the cement floor near soundlessly. "Go back to bed, kid."

Todd didn't need to be told again, but he did manage to shoot a glare in the guard's direction before he rolled back over and shoved his head under the flat prison-approved pillow. Dino wasn't even sure why they bothered to give them the pillows. They were only allowed one, and it was about as effective as sleeping on the fucking floor.

Frankly, he'd slept on the cell floor more than once.

It *was* more comfortable than the metal beds with their two-inch thick mattresses, the scratchy, thin sheets, and the garbage pillows.

At least a man knew what he was getting when he slept on a cement floor.

Dino hadn't realized how much he would miss sleeping in his bed.

Actually, that was a lie.

He didn't give a single shit about his bed.

He missed Karen's bed.

He missed that—*her*—a lot.

But since Dino knew where that rabbit hole would lead if he allowed himself to drift into those thoughts, he forced her name and face out of his mind. It was never good to be distracted in prison, he had come to learn, and Karen was most certainly a fatal distraction for Dino, no matter his circumstances.

"Come on," the guard said after the cell door had been unlocked and opened. "Mike is waiting for you in the private room."

Dino held out his arms, allowing the guard to cuff him so that he could be safely moved from one cell to another section of the prison for his meeting with his lawyer. When Mike came around, it wasn't the same thing as another inmate having one of their regular visiting days.

Mike was a lawyer, and that allowed Dino some privileges with the man. Privacy being one thing, but it was probably the biggest and most important thing.

Dino's meetings and any conversation with his lawyer were not allowed to be recorded or videoed by prison officials because of the attorney and client privilege laws. That meant instead of being shoved in front of a Plexiglas window with phones to chat through while guards sat at their backs and cameras monitored their every move, they were instead allowed a private room where Dino was still shackled to a table, but no one was privy to their conversations.

This would be only the third time Mike had actually come to visit Dino in the prison since he had entered all those many months ago. Mike had done his job as a court-appointed defense attorney on Dino's case, and once the judge had handed down his sentence, banged his gravel, and Dino was carted off to prison, the lawyer should have wiped his hands clean.

Mike didn't need to get involved with Dino after the case was closed.

For some strange reason, the man still did. He put money in Dino's prison account for him to use if he needed something, and every once in a while, he'd put in a request to one of the guards to have Dino call him just to check in on things.

Their relationship should have been limited to the charges and the sentencing.

Dino thought now it was almost ... *friendly*.

He wasn't quite sure how he felt about that.

Or Mike, for that matter.

Dino didn't have *friends*.

After all, when he had been on the outside, any friends he had made never lasted very long. Ben DeLuca had made damn sure of that.

"All right," the guard said as another barred and Plexiglas door was opened for them to walk through, "you've got thirty minutes, DeLuca, so don't waste it."

Dino didn't bother to thank the guard, but he did give the man a nod as he was shuffled into the private room and then shackled to the heavy metal table. Two bottles of unopened water sat in the middle of the table, and the guard cracked one open, sitting it in front of Dino before he took his leave.

He didn't touch the water, but only because he just wasn't thirsty. The thought had been nice, he simply wasn't in the mood. Fact was, their prison had it a lot better than others in the country did. For the most part, the guards were on the up, and they didn't do shoddy shit to cause the inmates any sort of trouble. Sometimes, they turned their cheek to a fight, but that was usually because the fool getting his head kicked in deserved it for whatever reason.

But mostly, the guards treated the inmates just fine.

Dino had to respect that.

He just didn't have to like them all that much.

Dino only waited another two minutes before the door buzzed and opened, Mike strolling in with a briefcase in hand and a smile on his face. The lawyer almost always smiled, though Dino wasn't quite sure what he had to be happy about, given where he currently was.

"Dino," Mike greeted, setting his case to the table and taking the seat across from Dino's. "Beautiful day outside."

"I wouldn't know," Dino replied, half-joking.

His seat, unlike Dino's, wasn't bolted down to the floor. Even the table was bolted down. It seemed like a bit much, but apparently it was all done in the name of safety. Who was he to make a fuss about something he barely had to be bothered with, anyway?

"How've you been?" the lawyer asked.

Dino shrugged, resting back in his chair as much as his shackles would allow. "Can't complain. They feed me. My cellmate doesn't talk me to death. The ceiling is keeping me entertained enough."

Mike cracked another smile. "You have jokes today."

"Not really a joke."

He'd only told the truth, after all.

Mike didn't have to know everything.

"Well, you're not shouting at me and threatening to feed me my teeth like the last time I was here, so I will take that as a good sign."

Dino didn't reply to that, but only because this time, it was Mike who was speaking truths.

Three times, Mike had come to visit Dino at the prison, and one of those times had been five months earlier, just a week and a half *after* Karen's surprise visit. For whatever reason, Dino had thought maybe—somehow—Mike had been involved in Karen showing up without warning. He threatened Mike with just about everything except throwing him in the ocean, to make sure Karen didn't show up like that again.

It could be a very costly mistake.

With visitors other than his lawyer, Dino's every single move was monitored. Someone was always watching. He didn't need the officials getting ahold of any sort of information that might lead them to Karen asking questions.

And then there was the other side of that equation, too.

His family, that was.

Ben, specifically.

It caused a striking pain to grow in his chest at the thought of something as simple as Karen coming to visit him in the prison. That her innocent gesture might put her on his uncle's fucking radar. Dino couldn't afford for that to happen.

Honestly, neither could Karen.

She just didn't know that was the case.

Dino knew how he must have seemed to her, all those months

ago when she came to see him—cold, distant, and unaffected at her presence.

That wasn't the case at all, at least, not on the inside.

It had taken every single ounce of willpower he had in his very being not to sit down at that visiting station and talk with her for as long as he possibly could; he'd wanted to apologize for everything that had happened, and for the shit he had put her through.

Dino had so very much to say to Karen.

He had a hell of a lot to apologize for.

Another year, he told himself.

He had one more year and then he would get every opportunity to fix the problems he had left hanging in the wind with Karen. He refused to even consider the fact that by the time he was out, she might not want a thing to do with him.

Dino would handle that when—or if—that came about.

For now, this would have to do.

"Did you do what I asked?" Dino questioned, his gaze flicking to Mike.

He'd allowed himself to think about Karen, and that was enough to hurt.

Dino didn't want to hurt.

Not right now.

Mike nodded. "I did. I contacted her through private means that wouldn't draw attention, explained who I was, and what you asked of her. She wasn't happy—actually, she told me not to ever contact her again."

Dino cleared his throat, surprised at Mike's description of Karen's response. She was not a rude woman, and she wasn't the type to be purposefully hateful to someone. But then again, maybe all of this had just been too much for her, and that was her way of acting out against it. He didn't know, and he really didn't have any reason to speculate on the whys of it all.

"What else?" Dino asked.

"Nothing, Dino. I did as she asked. I can't force information on her if she doesn't want to hear it. That's called harassment."

True.

Still …

"She hasn't come back since that first time," Dino said.

"Then she did what you wanted."

Dino wasn't sure if that was the case or not. Had she done what he requested, or had that one and only visit and his rejection been the final straw that broke her back where he was concerned?

God knew he wouldn't blame her if it was.

"But I did receive a letter to my office last week," Mike said, drawing in Dino's attention again.

"What does that have to do with me?"

Mike popped open his briefcase, pulling out a white envelope and passing it over. "I only opened it because it wasn't personally signed to go to you, but to my office, and to me. I figured she meant for it to somehow get to you ... maybe, say, in a way that the prison wouldn't get a hold of it first."

What?

Dino's confusion must have shown on his face, because Mike only chuckled when he asked, "She?"

"There's only one 'she' you're trying to keep away, isn't there?"

Dino didn't dignify that with a response.

Mike wasn't looking for one. "Open it. If you want, I can take it with me when I go, but I think you might want to keep it. At least, if it were me, I'd keep it. There's not much that could be identifiable, should someone stumble upon it."

He didn't have any idea what his lawyer was talking about, but the second he opened the envelope and tipped it over in his hand to empty the contents out, he understood perfectly fine.

A small six-by-four, colored photograph of a baby swaddled in blue with a matching wool cap stared up at him from his hands. For a long while, Dino simply stared at the photograph of the baby boy, unsure and wary in his heart.

But in his soul ... oh, there he felt *warm*.

Like he knew just by looking at the face of the child that this was *his* son.

His baby.

Dino sat there, staring at the photograph and saying nothing as he traced the features of his child with the tip of his index finger. He had so much guilt—so much regret. He'd missed too much already, he'd missed his baby's first day on earth.

He hadn't been sure he would even know how to *be* a father when he first learned about the pregnancy, but shit, he wanted to *try*.

He should be allowed to at least try for his son.

"Flip it over," Mike said. "She wrote on the back for you."

Dino did, finding Karen's familiar scrawl on the back of the photograph.

JD Martin, it read. *But I call him Junior.*

The baby's birthdate, just a week and a half earlier, was written underneath.

And then, under that, was something Dino hadn't expected.

I'll see you soon, Karen had written.

Nothing else.

Dino didn't need more.

It was enough.

This was perfect.

CHAPTER
6

Karen

JUNIOR barely batted an eye as the plane hit the runway a bit harder than Karen was expecting it to. She held on tighter to her six-month-old son, glancing out the porthole window to see the ground and runway flying by at a speed than damn near made her dizzy.

She didn't particularly like planes.

Flying wasn't her thing.

Thankfully, her son had done just fine on the trip from Chicago to California. Once he'd been fed, Junior had slipped off into one of his afternoon naps and the bit of bustle from the plane hadn't bothered him at all. She'd heard the horror stories about flying with babies, but her boy was proving those tales all wrong.

Kissing the side of her sleeping baby's head, Karen smiled.

Junior—though his birth certificate only stated simply "JD"—had been that way from the very moment he'd been born. He'd made his way into the world on the early morning of November 2nd, and he didn't make a fuss about it. He barely cried at all those first few days of his life, and Karen, being all by herself, had been damn near terrified.

She didn't know how to be a mother.

She didn't know how to suddenly care for this baby, who needed her twenty-four hours a day just to survive.

She didn't know anything.

But Karen learned.

Little by little. Day by day. She took each and every new thing in slowly, taking every minute she had with her son to let him teach *her* what he needed. Junior made it easy, but she wasn't quite sure how he had done it.

Karen still got to experience all the exhaustion of new motherhood and the craziness that came along with that. There were days that were harder than the rest, when she wished she didn't have to do everything alone. She struggled badly when Junior was only a month old and she handed the baby off to a respected daycare so that she could start work at a studio that needed an extra photographer.

Still, she did it.

Karen managed.

She moved forward, including getting a new apartment in Wicker that had more space and a small balcony she could sit on and rock her son when the weather was nice.

It helped that Junior was waiting for her to come pick him up from daycare every day, with his big smiles and brown eyes that damn near matched his father's. His tiny, chubby hands would fly up high as soon as he saw his mother come through the doors and his little fingers clenching over and over until she snatched him up and held him tight.

Oh, she adored her son.

Junior was *everything* that was right and good in her life.

Sometimes it hurt though, just to look at him and draw the similarities that he shared with his father. His light brown hair—almost a blond—came from Dino, as did his eyes, and the shape of his face. He shared his father's nose, but his mother's lips, but it was far more than just appearances, too.

Junior had seemed to take some of his father's personality as well. And he hadn't even met the man, yet.

For a long while, Karen had brushed off Junior's lack of interest in other people as just his age—that at only a few months old, he was too young yet to have much interest in others. His pediatrician did not think it was normal at all, the older doctor thought the boy needed to be interacting more with children.

Karen took him to the park.

He spent six hours a day in daycare.

How much more time with other children could he get?

No, the truth was simple.

Junior much preferred sitting off in a high chair or crib by himself with a pile of toys, or better yet, in his mother's arms listening to her talk. He was so fascinated by her voice, but he didn't much care for the attention of others.

Just like his dad.

Strange, how that worked.

It took another twenty minutes before the plane had taxied into its gate and the pilot came on the speakers to announce the end of the flight.

"Thank you for flying with us today," the flight attendant said as Karen passed, trying to shake her hand at the same time.

She gave the woman a smile. It was all she could offer, given she had a still-sleeping Junior in one arm, and his diaper bag she had used as a carry-on in the other arm. The flight attendant laughed and nodded, ushering Karen out of the plane.

It was only when the sudden noise of the airport started to filter down the long hallway of the gate did Junior finally stir on his mother's shoulder. She felt the baby's head lift, and his gentle puffs of breaths against her cheek as he peered all around.

Junior didn't like people.

But he liked to people watch.

"Sleepyhead, sleepyhead," Karen said in a singsong way, smiling when Junior squealed on her shoulder and started to wiggle. He was probably just realizing he had woken up in an entirely different place than he had fallen asleep in. "It won't be so cold here, Junior."

No, the cool May air from Chicago would not bother them at all in California.

Karen had taken two weeks off from work to bring her son to meet his grandparents. It had taken her his whole six months on earth, just to convince herself to come this far. She loved her parents—they loved her.

But from the very moment she had said she was going to Chicago as a young woman, they had disapproved. Not once had they hidden how they felt about it.

Karen had been positive her failures—her failed photography business, financial struggles, and even her pregnancy—would be the proof her parents needed to say the dreaded "I told you so."

She hadn't given her parents enough credit.

When she called to tell them about the pregnancy only shortly before the baby boy was born, her mother had demanded Karen allow her to come for the birth. It was too soon—there wasn't enough notice to get everything into place.

She'd promised to come there with the baby as soon as she could.

Six months later, here she was.

Focus would be mostly on Junior, she knew, and that would help. Karen just hoped her parents didn't ask too many questions about things she wasn't ready to tell just yet. Things like Dino, and exactly *how* Junior had come about.

"Here we go, baby," Karen murmured to her son as she stepped onto the escalator that would lead her to luggage pick up at the airport's Arrivals.

All her fears bled away the moment she saw her mother and father waiting at the bottom, just a foot away from the barrier that kept the people waiting from the people arriving. Her parents had been separated for years, rarely coming together for anything, but when they did, it was almost always for her.

It seemed that hadn't changed.

This wouldn't be so bad after all.

Even Junior started to smile.

Karen *loved* that.

"Look at him," Karen's mother said, her smile beaming. "He's having so much fun."

Lydia's happiness over her grandson's enjoyment of floating in the pool with his grandfather was damn near contagious. Karen had to admit, Junior did look awfully pleased with his swim trunks and flotation vest, as his grandfather walked him around the pool and he floated on his back.

"I haven't taken him to a pool," Karen admitted. "It's not been warm enough yet."

"An inside pool, maybe?" her mother asked.

"I'll have to find one and make time, seeing as how he likes this so much."

Lydia laughed. "You loved the water, too. Couldn't keep you out of it. Your father almost made me keep a lifejacket on you at all times, for fear you would find somewhere to *swim*. You didn't even know how to properly swim until you were four."

Karen hadn't known that little tidbit about her childhood, and found herself smiling at the unknown memory. "Really?"

"Yep." Lydia looked over at her, her smile growing softer. "I was worried you wouldn't come, Karen."

"Why wouldn't I come, Mom?"

Lydia shook her head, sighing. "You've just been so far away for so long, that's all."

"I'm here."

"Yes, *with* a baby."

Karen couldn't help but laugh. "I know—big change."

"I wish you would have told me sooner."

Yeah, she wished that, too.

"I thought you would be angry with me," Karen admitted.

Lydia placed a hand on her daughter's cheek, the action both tender and supportive. "I'm always going to be proud of you, Karen, no matter what. You're all grown up, so you get to make grown up decisions and I don't get much of a say. You're doing just fine."

Karen looked out, finding her son still smiling in the pool. "Sometimes, I think maybe I'm just really good at pretending to be okay—that I don't really know what I'm doing at all."

"Psht. All mothers feel that way for the first baby."

"Did you?"

Lydia shrugged. "All your life, even the day you walked out the door to do your own thing. It's what mothers do, Karen. We fret. We worry. We overthink. But in the end, we raise pretty amazing little creatures. It just takes us a while to figure that out."

Karen hadn't realized it, but she needed to hear those words.

Especially from her mother.

"Thanks," she whispered.

Lydia waved a hand as if to brush it all away. "It's nothing. Sometimes, we just need someone else to tell us that we're doing just fine and everything will be okay."

That was true enough.

However, Karen had meant to thank her mother for more than just her reassurances that she wasn't failing Junior in some way by being his mom.

"Actually, I meant for more than Junior." Karen pushed a few strands of her hair behind her ears, keeping her gaze on her son and not her mother. It was easier that way. "I was scared coming here would be awkward, or maybe a little bit sad. I didn't know how I would answer certain questions, if you starting asking things, or how you would feel about the answers I did give. You've done none of that, Mom, and neither has Dad. I really appreciate it."

Lydia cleared her throat and put the book she had been reading aside. "We're always going to be here, Karen. No matter what. If you have something you want to talk to us about, we'll always listen."

"I know."

"Do you have something you want to talk about?"

"Not particularly."

She did have a lot she wanted to talk about, but she just wasn't sure she should share. She fully believed her mother would be the shoulder to cry on or that supportive hand that held her up if she needed her to be.

Still, she had made a promise to herself.

Dino was not on the table during this visit.

She would not talk about Junior's father at all.

Karen didn't think it would be fair to Dino to out their history to her parents when she hadn't even given him the chance yet to clear it up to her.

Six more months, she told herself.

Karen had hoped Dino's sentence would be reduced, but it seemed like that wasn't going to be the case. She didn't know if it was because of who he was or the things he was affiliated with, but she'd been following along court documents and had occasionally called his lawyer's office for an update over the last couple of months.

Nothing had changed.

His release date was the same as it had always been.

"I thought I might be able to move on," Karen said before she could stop herself, "if I gave myself enough time and space."

Her mother glanced over at her, taking in those words for a long while before she finally responded with, "From Junior's father?"

Karen nodded quickly. "I was wrong, though. I keep going back in his direction in one way or another."

Checking the news for anything about the Chicago mob.

Calling his lawyer.

Reading any new court filings for his case.

Driving past his businesses.

Karen could pretend all she wanted that she was doing fine, that she didn't need Dino to be happy. And shit, maybe she didn't need him at all.

She was raising Junior alone as it were.

She was supporting herself.

She was just *fine*.

But she could be better.

She could be *happier*.

"I just don't know who he is," Karen said so softly her mother couldn't hear.

And sadly, that was still truer than she wanted to admit.

She'd read his letter over and over again. She kept the papers in her bedside table to pull them out and read them whenever she felt the urge, which was far more often than anyone could possibly know. He'd shown his heart in those words, his heart, past, and his pain, but reading it was not the same as hearing him say it.

Karen needed to hear it.

Six more months.

She thought, given their son and the way her heart hadn't quite let go yet, she owed Dino a chance to fix everything.

Didn't she?

CHAPTER
7

Karen

"HE'S still got a bit of the sniffles," Karen told the daycare worker as she handed eight-month-old Junior over to the woman's waiting arms. "I've tried everything."

"Still?"

"I know—the doctor wouldn't prescribe him anything, though. He kept saying something about his immune system and needing to build immunity."

Karen could tell just by the look on the woman's face that she thought the doctor was crazy. She didn't blame her because Karen also thought the doctor was a fool. Maybe it was time for a change in pediatricians for little J.

Ever since they had returned home from their trip to California, the baby boy had been plagued with one cold after another. Thankfully, he wasn't getting fevers or vomiting from whatever it was that wouldn't leave his little body, but it was getting tiring. Junior wasn't sleeping well, and he *loved* to sleep. That meant Karen also wasn't sleeping well.

"I'm sure he'll be fine," the daycare worker said, taking a tissue from Karen to wipe the baby's nose. "And he doesn't have much interest in the other kids, so it won't be hard to keep him in his own space and entertained."

Well, she supposed that was one good thing.

Karen didn't think Junior was all that contagious, given she hadn't gotten anything from him, but she understood the daycare's policy on sick children. She was damn lucky they had agreed to take Junior at all while she worked in the daytime. It was only *because* his doctor had written a note that explained the boy was suffering from non-contagious seasonal colds that the daycare allowed him in, with provisions.

She was grateful.

She couldn't afford time off from work.

"All right, say goodbye to your mom, J," the woman said.

Instantly, little Junior's eyes flew to Karen, knowing what those words meant. He sniffled a bit as Karen smoothed her hand over his head of soft hair and kissed his forehead.

"I love you, little man," she told him.

Junior smiled, his two top and bottom front teeth gleaming. The cold did nothing for his moods most days. He was still her bright ray of sunshine.

"Bye, bye, bye," he babbled, his chubby hand waving jerkily.

Karen smiled widely. "Bye, bye, bye, baby."

Junior could only speak a few words—things like hi, bye, mom, and a multitude of squeals to get what he wanted when he couldn't speak the words properly. Karen was quite proud of him, and given the way he toddled on his feet, attempting to stand against furniture already, she had no doubt her boy would be walking by the time his first birthday rolled around.

A pain stabbed in her heart at the thought.

Karen had all she could do to smile through it and wave to her son as she walked out of the daycare, ready to get on with her day so she could get it over with and get back to her son. But even as she tried to ignore that sudden swell of pain, it beat right through her focus, thrumming a little harder in her heart as she unlocked her car and sat behind the wheel.

Alone, it was easier to deal with.

Alone, she could let the tears fall if needed.

Karen took a deep breath, willing her emotions to calm. She'd been doing well lately, but the older Junior got, the closer to his first birthday he became, the more anxious Karen was becoming.

Dino would be released right around the baby's first birthday.

But he'd already missed *so* much.

It was a hard pill to swallow.

Karen had done her best to document their son's life, hoping that when she shared the memories with Dino, he wouldn't feel so lost. She also shared the few pictures she had taken of Dino with little Junior, hoping that the pictures would give him some connection to a man he had yet to meet.

Still, the pain beat on, thundering like a heavy drum in her soul.

Karen just didn't have the time to focus on all of that. Not when she had to be at work in twenty minutes, her rent was due, and Junior was running low on his favorite snacks.

This was how she made it through the day.

Tasks to complete.

Each one took focus and time.

Then the day was over, and she could turn her attention to the next day.

It was easier that way.

Karen pulled her car out onto the road, sliding into traffic easily and making good time as she headed toward the studio where she worked. She had only just parked in the lot of the studio when her phone rang. Not wanting to be late, she picked up the call as she strolled across the lot, heading for the back entrance of the studio.

"Hello?" Karen said into the phone.

"Miss Martin, this is Mike Hardy giving you a call. Dino's—"

"Dino's lawyer. I know. You don't need to introduce yourself to me every time you call, Mike," she reminded him gently.

The lawyer laughed. "So you keep telling me."

Their words almost implied they chatted often, but the truth was simple. They rarely had contact at all. Mike had contacted her once after Karen had mailed in the picture of her newborn son, hoping the lawyer would get the hint and deliver it to Dino. He'd wanted to make sure that was her intention, and when she confirmed it was, he assured her that he would bring it to Dino as soon as he possibly could.

Despite feeling as though she shouldn't ask, during that phone call Karen had requested the lawyer keep her up-to-date on anything that might be important regarding Dino, like his release efforts and whatnot.

The lawyer had promised to do so.

He'd only called one other time—to say Dino would not be getting an early release.

This was the third call she had gotten from the man, and she didn't have a clue what he would be calling for, considering Dino still had another four months and possibly a week or two before his release would come up.

"Why the call?" Karen asked as she pulled open the back door of the studio. "He's not getting out for a while yet, right?"

She could already hear the other two photographers chatter down the hallway, telling her they were getting set up for the scheduled shoots they had that day. A couple of softball team photos, and some family bookings. The place did decent business, and having more than one photographer on hand meant they could book several shoots over the day and work in tandem.

"Dino's release has not changed," the lawyer replied.

Karen's heart stuttered for a second, a slight sliver of fear crawling up her spine. "Did something happen?"

"Oh, no. Not at all. I'm sorry, I should have said that right away. This is … uh, well, it's rather good. Dino had called to make a request regarding some things he wanted to do, and thought maybe I could help him out with it all."

"Those requests involve me?" Karen asked.

"You *and* the baby," Mike corrected.

"Oh."

"I'd much rather explain it in person, rather than over the phone. It's a lot to go over and whatnot. Dino and I have been working on the details for a couple of months, and things have finally fallen into place. The ink is dry, so to speak, and things look good."

Karen was more confused than she wanted to admit.

She was also a little wary about meeting with the lawyer, if only because Dino had made it quite clear before he entered prison that he didn't want her involved with people who might expose her to the other side of his life, and the people there. She didn't entirely understand why, but she trusted his judgement.

It was well known the lawyer was working for Dino.

Would those people be watching him?

So, yeah, she hesitated.

"A quick cup of coffee and a drive is all it would take," the lawyer prodded when Karen stayed quiet.

Karen peered down the hall, seeing just the shadow of one of her employers back at the very end as the woman moved between studio rooms. "I'm working right now, so I can't say yes at the moment."

"Later?"

"I have to pick the baby up at daycare at four."

Mike sighed heavily. "Listen, Karen, I know you probably want to keep a distance from Dino and—"

On that, Karen had to stop the man. "No offence, but you don't know *anything* regarding how I feel about Dino or where he and I stand."

He cleared his throat quickly. "You're right—I apologize. This is important to him, though, and he's made a great effort to have it done and ready for you. Not an easy thing being where he is, let me just say."

"I have no idea what you're talking about."

"I'm aware. Can you get off work a little early?"

"I can try," Karen obliged.

She wasn't promising a thing. Her boss could be difficult, though the woman had given her a good job and paid her well. Karen was not about to complain.

"Call me back if you can. I will meet you anywhere you want, Karen."

"Sounds like a plan."

Karen pulled her car into the lot of a tiny café that was only ten minutes away from her work. She didn't bother to shut off her car, as she had parked right beside the man meeting her there, and he was already leaning against his own black Toyota.

She rolled down the window when he smiled, and then accepted the to-go cup of coffee he handed her.

"Thanks," Karen said, taking a sip. "My fuel for the rest of this day."

Mike laughed. "I know the feeling. Lawyers live off of caffeine and take-out."

Karen made a face. "Tell me about it."

"Gotta do what we gotta do. Care to take a drive?"

She checked the time, noting she only had an hour and a half before she had to pick up her son. "How long is it going to be?"

"A half hour there."

And a half hour back, she knew.

Shit.

"Could I follow you? Just in case I have to come back early and you need to stay behind or whatever. Daycare for the baby, remember?"

Mike shrugged like it didn't make a difference to him. "Sure."

Nearly a half hour later, Karen almost missed when Mike turned his blinker on to signal he was turning off the highway to leave the outskirts of the city when an exit ramp came up. She'd been following behind him for so long that the radio and the passing cars had put her into a trance of sorts.

This was why Karen hated driving, though it was a necessary evil.

She didn't recognize the rural area Mike directed them through, as she hadn't visited outside of Chicago on this side of the city, but it looked quiet … and certainly private.

It was only when Mike had put on his blinker again, turning off onto a long, paved driveway that seemed to go on and on with no end in sight that Karen really did stop to take notice of where they were. She didn't have time to take in the beautiful driveway and trees lining either side before a large, Victorian-style home came into view, taking all of her attention.

Karen parked her car, still staring at the house.

Mike had already gotten out of his vehicle, and he patiently waited for her to do the same. She hadn't taken her eyes off the large entrance with its massive pillars once as she came to stand at the lawyer's side.

"Well, what do you think?" Mike asked. "Thirty acres, private, three-level home with attached garage."

Karen just gaped.

Had Dino done what she thought he had done?

How?

"It's … beautiful," Karen admitted.

"He thought you might like it," Mike said with a smile. "'Homey,' he said. You appreciate that kind of thing, apparently."

Karen still wasn't sure she knew what was happening. "Did he buy this?"

"Signed the final papers yesterday, actually. Only a few of his accounts haven't been frozen, and those were ones related to businesses the feds haven't touched yet. We assume they will after he's released, because they'll be opening up everything in an attempt to get him pinned down again."

All Karen had heard in those statements was that Dino might be going back to prison after he was out.

She really didn't want to think about that.

"I can't take this," Karen said, more to herself than to Mike. "This is too much."

"He thought you might feel that way, and if you want, you can wait. You don't have to take it right now. After all, his name is on the deed, not yours. Dino just wanted to show you, in a way he was capable of, that he is trying to plan beyond his current situation— that he does want to be … well, a family, I suppose."

Yeah, Karen got that.

"I don't think I could just move in here without …"

She didn't finish her sentence, letting it hang in the wind.

Mike nodded like he didn't need her to continue. "I get it. There's one other thing, though."

Karen looked to the lawyer, warier than ever. "What's that?"

"The cabin on the lake he owns—he said you would know what he was talking about without me needing to go into details."

Her mouth went dry.

Of course she knew.

It was where she had fallen in love with Dino.

"What about it?" Karen dared to ask.

Mike pulled a large envelope from the inside pocket of his blazer, handing it over to Karen with a smirk. "Non-negotiable, the property is signed over to you. He's not arguing about it, it's an asset he doesn't want claimed—the papers make it look like it was sold to someone else, who then put it into an auction, where you've then purchased the home and property. It's all yours, Karen, just sign before we leave."

Karen was *thunderstruck*.

"But—"

Mike gave her a look, quieting her. "This one is already done, and he's not changing anything about it. He's going to take care of his son in one way or another, whether you want to be with him or you don't. This is one way he's chosen to do that. Sign and the lake property is yours."

How in the hell was she supposed to say no to that?

CHAPTER 8

Dino

ONCE again, Dino found himself sitting across a table he was shackled to as he listened to his lawyer chatter away about the events of the week before. Mike was a temporary reprieve to the quiet hell that he would need to return to in a few short minutes.

Dino tried to savor the conversation as much as he could before it was over.

"She signed the papers for the lake property," Mike said, "but she had a few choice words to say to me as she did it."

Dino chuckled, unable to hold it back. "Is that so?"

"She doesn't seem like the type to just grin and bear it."

"She isn't."

Karen was far from that type of woman.

She also wasn't the type to let a man take care of her, even if the reason why Dino had done what he did regarding the lake house was to her and his son's best benefit. He had already figured Karen wouldn't be pleased at first about it all, but like she usually did, she would find out a way to work through it.

She loved that property.

He remembered the way she had lit up the night they had arrived.

Amazement and joy all rolled into one.

Dino smiled to himself at the memory, pleased that Karen had taken the property off his hands without too much of a fight. She deserved it—the place was perfect for her, even if it was a little further from the inner parts of the city than she would have liked.

She needed a home—his son needed a home.

The other home he had purchased was one he hoped Karen would eventually warm up to, if maybe they could one day be an actual family together. He'd bought it on a whim, but knew it was more than likely something she would refuse.

So, he'd given her a second option.

Even if it wasn't really an option at all.

"The feds still might seize the house," Mike said quietly.

Dino nodded. "But they might not. A few of my accounts are still open. That all looks good. I haven't had another visit from an agent wanting to talk, so that's a bonus point for me. I'll have time before I'll have to worry about it all."

"Don't stick your head too far in the clouds, Dino."

Oh, he wasn't stuck up there.

Dino was firmly shackled right to the goddamn ground.

"Probably better she didn't take the house and signed the lake property deed," he admitted after a stretch of silence passed between him and his lawyer.

"Why not?" Mike asked.

"The feds can't seize something that isn't mine to begin with, I suppose."

"That's true, but I don't think that's the only reason you brought it up."

Mike was astute.

Dino had to give the lawyer that credit.

"I don't trust that some of the documents that were stolen from me a year ago aren't going to be used again at some point," Dino said, resting back as far as he could in the chair. "And since I know my uncle took the paperwork, that means he's got eyes on me and my shit. He probably just picked up on the fact—or he soon will—that I bought a house."

Dino hadn't even thought of this stuff before purchasing the house. He'd only focused in on the fact he wanted—*needed*—to do something for Karen and his son so that they could be taken care of in some small way. He also wanted to show Karen that he was planning ahead, for her, him, their child, and whatever she might want in the future.

She made the calls.

She always would.

It was only now that he realized it might not have been a good thing to make such a large purchase—a house worth three quarters of a million dollars—and possibly raise the suspicions of his uncle *if* by chance Ben was watching Dino's financials.

It certainly hadn't been an easy thing to do while locked up.

Mike had helped a lot, and had done most everything Dino needed him to do, as long as he could do so in a legal way. The guy was a great lawyer, even if he was just a public defender. Dino thought Mike was wasting his time in that regard, and he needed to get himself in somewhere he could shine.

Although, none of that was important at the moment.

"She won't be anywhere near that house," Mike assured.

Dino didn't know if that was enough, though. "She might not need to be."

"The lake property isn't attached to you, and it does look like it was just auctioned off, and that she was the one who happened to put in the right bid. Don't sweat the small stuff."

That was the problem.

Dino didn't think this was small at all.

And to be safe ...

"Keep a distance from her," Dino said, "just in case. She's signed the paperwork and it's all changed over now, you've been paid, so there's no reason to keep contact, right?"

"She's not my client, Dino."

"That's not what I said, Mike."

Mike sighed. "She wants me to let her know when your official release date is."

Dino shrugged. "It'll be in the news."

The lawyer didn't disagree.

That was that.

Clang. Clang. Clang.

Dino's eyes popped open to the annoying sound of metal

hitting metal just outside of his cell. He barely had time to roll over before the sound started up again.

Fucking guards.

"Up and at 'em, boys," the guard shouted. "Showers for block A in ten minutes, breakfast for block B in fifteen minutes."

The guard shouted a few more things, but Dino wasn't paying the man any mind. The routine didn't change, and it wasn't about to start changing any time soon. Of that, he was positive. Routine and three meals a day was just about the only things the prison guaranteed its inmates.

Dino pushed off his bunk to stand just as the guard came into view of his cell door. Under his arm, the guard held a newspaper, and stopped to peer in at Dino and a still-sleeping Todd.

"Wake your cellmate up," the guard said.

"I'm not a babysitter."

The man just scowled. "He'll miss the showers."

What a sad fucking thing that would be.

Cold water, soaps that stank *and* hurt the skin, and thirty other inmates plus ten guards watching you clean yourself with no privacy in sight?

Yeah, that'd be a fucking *shame.*

"Oh, and I got something for you, DeLuca," the guard said. "Somebody asked me to pass it along in the breakroom."

Dino's brow lifted in curiosity, but he didn't move from his position. While most of the guards treated the inmates okay, there were a few that just rubbed him the wrong way. A man of his sort—that lived the life he had led for many years—could pick up that sort of thing from another man without needing much confirmation.

Some of these guards were not to be trusted.

They could be bought if needed, from the outside or the inside.

Dino didn't need to be told to *know.*

"Here," the guard said, sticking the newspaper he'd been holding through the bars of the cell. "Well, fucking take it."

He still didn't move.

With a harsh sigh, the guard dropped the newspaper to the cell floor, and started off again, moving onto the next cell without a look back.

Dino eyed the paper on the floor, wondering what in the hell that show was all about. Todd had finally started to grumble and shift on the bottom bunk behind Dino, and it was only when the kid was fully awake and standing did he, too, notice the newspaper.

"What's that?" Todd asked.

"I don't know."

"Shouldn't you check it?"

"For what?"

Todd's brow furrowed. "I don't know—the news?"

Dino didn't trust a fucking soul, his life had taught him not to. And he didn't think the guard dropping that stupid newspaper off like nothing was amiss was just random happenstance, either. He wasn't sure he was ready to find out just what might be *inside* the paper that someone had wanted him to see.

And just *who* was that someone, anyway?

It wasn't like Dino had made friends with any of the guards.

"Jesus, you're strange," Todd mumbled before he scooped up the paper and slammed it into Dino's chest.

He caught the item before it could fall from his grasp. Unfolding the paper in his hands had been a mistake, because as soon as he did, he saw the headline and understood *exactly why* the guard had dropped the paper off to him.

Someone wanted him to know something important …

Someone thought he should see …

Dino read the headline again and again, desperately trying to find the error that would tell him he wasn't actually reading it right at all.

The headline remained the very same.

Public Defender Mike Hardy Murdered Outside Office!

Dino blinked again.

The headline didn't change.

"Thirty minutes," the guard told Dino.

"Yeah, got it."

He sat down in the hard chair, facing the Plexiglas wall and staring down a man he wished he never had to see again.

Ben DeLuca looked entirely too comfortable sitting in his own chair, a slight smile curving his lips and his suit and tie a pristine black. Much like his eyes—coal black and unfeeling. So fucking cold.

Dino might have been surprised to see his uncle sitting there requesting a visitation with him, but he wasn't. Not at all.

It'd been only a week since Mike had been killed, and in that time, Dino had lots of quiet moments to think everything through and put more than enough together to prepare for this. Because he had known it would come.

With Ben, things like this always came.

Ben waved at the phone, and though the last thing he wanted to do was have any sort of conversation with Ben DeLuca, Dino grabbed his phone and put it to his head. The sound of his uncle's breaths crackling through the speakers just pissed him off.

He had no doubt Ben had been the one to kill Mike.

He didn't know *why*, but he figured that information would come in due time.

So, yeah, it pissed him off to hear the breaths of a man who wasn't worthy enough to shine the shoes of the man he'd killed, no matter the reason.

"You look well," his uncle said into the phone.

Dino shrugged, refusing to give his uncle any hint to his anger or even the fear he felt that Ben might know *something* about Karen or his son. "It's prison—all we can do is eat, work out, and sleep. It's good for the soul, you know."

Ben chuckled drily. "I'm sure."

"What do you want, Ben? You haven't come to visit me since that day in the jail. Say what you've come to say and leave me alone to finish this sentence out."

"Punishment," his uncle corrected swiftly. "Your *punishment.*"

No, Dino wasn't going to play that game with his uncle.

He'd worry about that when he was out of his current hell.

"Quite a little friend you made in that lawyer, hmm?" Ben asked.

Dino didn't blink.

He kept his expression unreadable, cold like his uncle's.

Ben had done this to him, after all.

He'd wanted this for a nephew, not one that *cared.*

"You know you can't have outsiders doing business for you," Ben went on, seemingly unbothered by Dino's lack of silence. "Playing in your accounts and seeing things they shouldn't be seeing. It's unacceptable."

"Or was it the fact I was doing something without you getting to dig all through it?" Dino asked coolly.

Ben smiled again, cruel and violet in a flash. "Same thing, isn't it?"

"I had him buy me a house and sell another."

"But why not use someone we both know and trust? You didn't want me to know you were doing it, you're still under some sort of impression that you're free to do whatever you want to do," Ben said, glancing down at his watch. "This was a reminder, Dino, and nothing more, just in case you needed one, and it certainly seemed like you did."

"A reminder of *what*?"

"I am always watching. Remember that."

How was he supposed to forget it?

Every one of his monsters was sitting just two feet away behind a Plexiglas window wearing a pleased smile and a three-thousand-dollar suit.

Dino wasn't about to forget any of that.

Ben, however, hadn't mentioned a thing about Karen or Dino's son. He acted like he didn't know about them. Dino would take that as a battle won. He was sorry that Mike had needed to die for it, though.

Sometimes that was just how shit worked.

They didn't get any say in that at all.

CHAPTER 9

Karen

"HERE, you take the cake," Corrine said, handing the platter over to Karen.

Somehow, she managed to get the camera in her hands sat down on the table, and balanced the cake at the same time, without losing it all over the studio floor. Her boss—Corrine—did one last check of the cake to make sure it still looked perfect. The face of Junior's favorite cartoon character had been piped with colorful icing while the words "Happy Birthday, J!" had been written in fancy scrawl across the bottom.

"Ready?"

Karen nodded. "Light the candles and I'll take it in."

"I'll get lots of pictures, promise."

She almost laughed.

Getting enough pictures was not her concern today. She had two wonderful photographers she worked with that she was lucky enough to also call her friends. And when the week before, Karen had admitted she hadn't planned anything for Junior's first birthday, the women took control of the situation and promised to do something for both Karen and her son that would be memorable.

Messy, but memorable.

It wasn't that she hadn't wanted to do something for Junior's birthday, but really, Karen didn't know *what* to do. Outside of work, she didn't have a lot of people that she spent time with on a personal level. She hadn't made friends with any of the parents at J's daycare center, and the one-year-old boy didn't have much interest in other kids.

What exactly could Karen do for a party or something of the sort?

No, she had just planned on getting Junior a cake, some balloons for him to play with, and a gift or two for him to open. Just him and her together.

That's what their whole life had been, anyway.

Corrine quickly lit the candles on the cake, and then shooed Karen toward the studio room where Junior was waiting with Kathy, the other photographer they worked with.

Instantly, the baby's eyes found his mother when she walked into the room, and he lit up with a wide, toothy grin. He still wasn't walking quite yet, but he got around just fine by crawling, so that was what he did. The toys and Kathy, lost his attention as he scrambled toward his mother and the cake she held.

"Momma!"

"It's your happy birthday," she told him.

Junior grabbed onto the legs of her dark-wash jeans, using her body to steady himself as he stood. "Ma, Ma, Ma."

Each one of his crows was punctuated by a small tug of his hands to her jeans, and he bounced on his heels. The cute little red bowtie he wore helped to set off the dress pants and white shirt ensemble that was about to be stained and ruined.

Karen smiled, unable to help the joy she always seemed to feel whenever she was in the presence of her son. He had a way of making her feel like she was the most important thing to grace his presence. As though she was the one person in the world who made him happy, and he didn't need anything or anyone else.

"Okay, J," Kathy said, snatching him up, even when he howled at her for taking him away from his mother. "Time for a sugar high, little man."

Karen laughed. "I doubt he'll eat that much of it."

"Never give kids enough rope to hang themselves, as the saying goes."

She wasn't quite sure that was how the saying went, but then again, Kathy didn't have kids so she was the type who spoiled everyone else's children and then gave them back when she'd had enough.

Kathy sat Junior in front of the large birthday backdrop, and the baby instantly tried to go back to where his mother was standing. The baby and the adult wrangled back and forth for a good minute before Corrine came into the room, her camera already at the ready to catch the action first hand.

"We ready?" Corrine asked.

"I don't have to clean the mess after, right?" Karen questioned.

Corrine shot her a look from the side. "You clean the baby. We'll handle the rest of the mess."

She could do that.

"Ready."

"Ouch, he bit me!" Kathy said as she put Junior in front of the backdrop once more.

Karen wasn't surprised, if only because that was a new thing for her son, and she'd had a couple of complaints from his daycare about it over the last week. "It's a thing he's doing."

"Should bite him back."

"Step back," Corrine muttered, "he just wants his mom and his cake."

Karen squatted down to Junior's level, and all over again, his tantrum was seemingly done, his pearly white teeth flashing in a grin at the sight of his mother. She sat the cake in front of him, helped him to blow on the big number one candle resting in the very middle, and then waited to see what the baby would do.

Junior did nothing.

"Come on, J," Karen said. "It's cake, baby."

He stared between the cake, and his mother, never moving a muscle.

"Stick one of his hands in the frosting and then move out of the way," Corrine suggested.

"But—"

"Trust me, it works every time. They just need a taste to understand."

Karen went ahead and grabbed Junior's chubby little hand in her own, and then dragged the tips of his tiny fingers through the top of the cake. Then, she put his hand close to his mouth, his pink lips opening automatically at the sight of something colorful on his fingers that he might be able to eat.

Babies were a lot of things, but constant and predictable were the most common traits they shared. Junior was *no* exception to that rule. At a year old, he was still smack dab in the middle of the stage where if he found something on the floor that even looked remotely edible, it was going into his mouth. And if someone put something in his hand that looked like it might taste good, he was going to try and eat that, too.

Karen found herself on her knees, trying to coax Junior to open his mouth, far more than she wanted to admit. This was one stage in her baby's life she would be glad to see go. It scared her sometimes.

"See," Corrine said, a smugness to her tone.

Sure enough, the second Junior had gotten a taste of the frosting on the cake, his brown eyes widened, and he grabbed for more. Karen took a step back, giving Corrine lots of room to take shots of the baby and his first year cake smash. Junior no longer cared that Karen was more than a few feet away from him because his focus was only on shoving as much cake and frosting into his sweet face as he could.

By the time he was finished, he was covered in pieces of chocolate cake, and his skin and clothes were stained from top to bottom with blue and red frosting. The floor looked like someone had stuck a bomb inside the cake and it had blown up spectacularly.

Junior sucked happily on his fingers, his other hand smacking the chocolate mess he'd made on the floor, as Corrine took her final shots.

"These are going to be great," she told Karen.

Karen had no doubt. They would certainly be fun to hang up once she had the prints. The hard part would be deciding whether or not she was going to hang them in the apartment, or the lake property.

She still hadn't made a choice on whether or not to move.

The place was hers, sure, but still ...

Karen just didn't know what to do.

"Now comes the fun part," Kathy said.

Karen shot her a look over her shoulder. "The cake wasn't fun?"

Corrine snorted. "No, now we have to clean."

Ah.

Yeah.

That.

Karen couldn't find a clean place on her son to kiss, except for the very top of his head. "Happy birthday, J."

His sticky hand smacked her cheek gently, probably leaving a chocolate and frosting J-sized print behind. Karen didn't even mind. The happiness in her son's eyes was the highlight of her day, and seeing how much fun he'd had doing a simple cake smash to celebrate his birthday helped to ease some of the sadness she had been feeling that hadn't quite let up. She'd wanted to share this day with someone else, but it was impossible, and that left her a little blue.

Junior's smile made it all okay.

At least for a little while.

After all, reality was never too far behind.

"No, you have to keep that on, J," Karen told her son, fixing his hat for the tenth time since they'd arrived at the park.

The baby scowled up at his mother as she tied the strings down around his chin in an effort to force him to keep the hat on. The mid-November air was chilly, and while there wasn't snow on the ground just yet, she could feel it all around her. It wouldn't be long before the white flakes started falling, covering Chicago in ice and cold for months.

Karen wasn't looking forward to that very much. It would mess up her schedules, and probably take Junior's outside time down to practically nothing at all. Sometimes, the baby caught a cold at the slightest winds, so she wasn't too keen on taking him out very much in the coming winter.

Junior liked the park, though, so she was trying to get him there as much as she possibly could before the snow started coming. He didn't do much except crawl around and try to climb on the play equipment, but he still enjoyed it. Sometimes, he would let his mother push him in the swings if he was in the mood for it, but mostly, he crawled off to find whatever sticks or stones looked appealing enough for him to stick into the pockets of his coat.

Karen leaned against the metal fence, tucking her own coat closer to her body to combat the chill. She watched J as he pushed himself up to a standing position, and tried to take a step forward. In his heavy boots, he struggled and fell, catching himself easily.

He didn't try to walk again, though, instead crawling to where the sandbox was.

Another one of his favorite spots in the park.

Knowing her son would be fine to play, and seeing as how the park was mostly empty of children, given it was a school day and not even noon, she found one of the park benches to sit on and try to relax.

While her attention was on her son and making sure he didn't wander off or stick something in his mouth, her mind was somewhere else entirely.

He should be out.

His sentence is served.

Is he out?

Those questions plagued her as she watched J throw a handful of sand up into the air.

Karen had asked one thing of Dino's lawyer, and that was to let her know the official date of his release. She had never gotten that phone call, and for good reason. When she called the office where Mike Hardy had worked, she learned exactly why she hadn't been contacted by the lawyer.

He was dead.

Murdered, apparently.

It made her sick all over.

"Careful!" Karen shouted to her son as Junior balanced on the edge of the sandbox and leaned forward, trying to grab something from the ground. "Sit down, J!"

The baby plopped down on his butt with a laugh, but didn't turn to look at his mother. So was their routine when they came to the park—he was always trying to get into some kind of trouble, and Karen damn near had a heart attack every time. She was sure the older he got, the worse it would be for her.

She still loved him for it.

He was far more adventurous than she had remembered being as a child.

Karen wasn't quite sure what it was that made her feel like

someone was watching her, but the hair on the back of her neck prickled. Strangely, it wasn't a bad thing. She didn't feel ... unsafe like maybe she should have.

She didn't even get the chance to turn and see if someone else had parked in the park's lot before she felt his presence. And she *knew* in an instant exactly who it was.

Maybe it was the way his shadow fell over hers, the sizeable shape swallowing her whole. He had always been larger than her, making her feel so small but so important in his world.

Maybe it was the sound of his throat clearing, something he'd done time and time again when he felt like he was inserting himself into her time and life and didn't deserve to be there, so he tried to give her warning.

Maybe it was the way her heartrate picked up.

Or the shaky breath she released.

Karen couldn't pinpoint exactly what it was that explained how she knew, she just *did.*

Dino.

"I met a girl once," he said behind her, "and she only had to talk to make me smile."

Karen didn't know what to say, but she knew he was talking about her. "Oh?"

"Fascinating woman, really."

"I bet."

"I fucked it up, though."

Karen blinked, her vision cloudy from gathering wetness. "You don't know that."

"Don't I?" he asked softly. "I'm still trying to figure out how to tell her I'm sorry."

Jesus.

Karen patted the seat beside hers on the bench. "Sit."

Dino didn't make her tell him again.

CHAPTER 10

Dino

SETTING the small Styrofoam package at his side on the bench, Dino settled into his seat, torn between giving the woman at his side all of his attention, and looking out at the toddling baby playing at the edge of the sandbox.

Dino had so many questions.

He had so much he wanted to say.

Right then, all he could do was *stare*.

"When did you get out?" Karen asked.

Dino cleared his throat, getting out of his head and back to the present. "A couple of days ago."

He didn't offer the rest of the story, because frankly, there wasn't much to tell. That was probably the saddest part. He'd come out of the prison in a sort of haze with a brown paper bag under his arm of all the possessions he had gone into the prison with. It'd taken him an entire ten minutes of standing outside the gates, staring down the walkway, before he realized no one was waiting there for him.

No one to pick him up.

No one to take him home.

He'd come out entirely alone.

Much the same way he had gone in.

"You didn't think to call?" Karen asked. "Maybe let me know you would be coming around?"

Dino chuckled. He heard the annoyance in her voice, but the

relief was far clearer to him. She wasn't mad—not about him showing up like this. Of that, he was most sure.

"Had to find you first," Dino explained. "You changed your number, and then you moved. I didn't have that new info."

Karen passed him a look, her brown eyes holding his gaze strong for the briefest second before she dropped it. "It didn't take you very long."

Understatement.

He'd actually found Karen quite quickly.

It'd only taken a look in the phone book, then a call for an address, and finally, a drive. Of course, nothing was ever simple, and while he had found her and his son easily enough after being released, Dino still had to be careful.

Especially now, he had to be extremely careful.

Karen was only *now* finding out Dino was released, but she was the exception to the rule. The Outfit—his family and uncle—already knew. He hadn't gone home yet, not in the proper respect, and he hadn't shown face to his uncle or his boss, but that would happen.

Soon.

Or ... when he felt like it.

Dino made a special effort to disappear after he'd come out of the prison, not wanting to make much of a fuss or draw too much attention from the police, FBI, and especially *not* Ben DeLuca. He had more important things to be doing, rather than playing pretend for those people.

Things like Karen.

And his son.

So he disappeared, but he had zero doubt that Ben wasn't already demanding someone find him.

Dino was hoping for a couple of days.

A little bit of time ...

Anything.

"Why that name?" Dino asked. "JD Martin. Why that, Karen?"

She looked over at him again, and he stared right back at her, not letting her drop his gaze that time around. He'd waited so long for her, hoping all the while that she had been out in the world, waiting on him, too. Seeing her, being close to her, brought up all those feelings and memories he had suppressed while in prison.

Things that he felt would have led him down a rabbit hole of pain.

The way her eyes sparkled—how her soul shined.

The slight curve of her lips, and her brilliant smile.

Her heart—how it beat; how he'd broken it.

All of that rushed through his emotions like a wrecking ball, never giving him enough time to think one thing over before the next was smashing through his veins, too, ready to devastate him with the impact.

Dino didn't care.

He never minded.

He let each one of them crash into him, and take him under.

"I still love you," he told Karen softly. "I never realized just how much until I didn't have anything to do but *think* about how much I love you. I'm sorry I didn't tell you properly, and that I left it just hanging there for so long, Karen."

She blinked, slivers of wetness coating her bottom lashes before the tears fell down her cheeks, making track lines for pathways on her skin. Still, she didn't make a move to wipe the tears away; she didn't hide her emotions.

It was such a foreign sight to Dino.

He'd spent his whole life hiding his emotions and the way he truly felt from others. He had been taught never to be seen as weak by those around him; he'd been taught to hide the weaknesses someone else might exploit for their own benefit.

He'd had no other choice.

And then Karen had come into his life like a spring shower—fresh, new, and revitalizing. A spectacular life, the most beautiful soul. She was so entirely innocent to the things he was and the actions he committed. So, he had held on to that innocence, liking how the brightness of her life colored up the darkness of his own.

She wasn't like him.

She was so much better than him.

Dino couldn't ever let her go.

Not when she was as perfect as she was.

"You didn't even let me answer your first question," Karen whispered.

Dino shrugged. "We've got some time."

"Do we?"

"A couple of days, maybe."

Karen frowned. "And then what?"

He'd spent a lot of time lying to her before. And not necessarily purposeful lies meant to hurt her, but he'd omitted facts, simply to keep her naive to the other side of his life and the mafia business he didn't want her getting mixed up in.

Dino knew that probably wouldn't fly with Karen this time around.

That was, if she gave him another round.

"Then I have to make face with the important people in my business and get back to life," he explained honestly.

Karen folded her hands onto her lap, but not before Dino saw the tiny tremor rocking through them. "And what about us? Aren't we important people to you?"

"Hey."

She didn't look at him.

In fact, she turned a bit, angling her body farther from him.

Dino couldn't have that. "Karen, hey. Look at me."

Not waiting for permission, Dino slipped his hand around her clenched fists. Silently, he worked through the knot her hands had become, until he had her palm pressed to his and their fingers woven tightly together. The warmth and softness of her skin soaked into the rough coldness of his, another one of their stark contrasts that he adored.

She warmed him.

She made him feel alive.

"You're the *most* important people to me," he assured firmly.

"But you just said you have to go back—get back to life, right?"

A bitterness coated her words.

Dino didn't begrudge Karen her feelings.

"This is for life," he told her, trying to convey the suffocating expectations and rules of the life he lived without putting her front row and center for it. It was a hard thing to do when the person who needed to understand had never lived in that sort of way before. "I'm always going to be the man affiliated to the mafia—the criminal with a fucking target on his back."

"But—"

"That doesn't mean I wanted this, Karen."

She stilled, her fingers clenching tight around his. "But here you are."

"Someone didn't give me a choice. I'm trying to make the best of what I have—I finally have a reason to do that now, because before, I was just going day to day doing what I had to since I didn't have a reason not to."

Karen sighed shakily. "I don't know who you are, Dino."

"You do, I just forgot to mention a few things along the way."

"You think?"

"I never said I was perfect."

Karen laughed lightly, the sound coming off like tinkling wind chimes. "You know, that's funny. It's all in perspective, Dino, and I don't think you have the right perspective of yourself to be giving that kind of opinion."

"I *know* you don't think I'm perfect."

He almost wanted to dare her to deny it.

Karen didn't.

"In Japan, anything broken that can be repaired is often done so with gold. The culture believes that in doing so, it adds a beautiful piece of history to the object's story. Nothing is ever really broken that way, only more beautiful, with a bit more to tell."

Dino eyed her from the side. "I'm a man, not an object."

"The sentiment is the same. It's all about perspective."

"I don't know how to begin to repair all the broken parts of me," he said quietly.

Karen moved a little closer to him on the bench until they were pressed together and her head was resting on his shoulder. "You started out in the right way—coming here, talking to me, and all of that. This is a good start, Dino."

"How much longer do I have to go?"

"A ways."

Dino nodded. "You still didn't answer my first question."

"His name?"

"Yeah, that."

Dino looked out to see the baby had climbed over the side of the sandbox, and was now staring in their direction, his focus stuck firmly on the man at his mother's side. The baby tipped his head to the side, a familiar brown gaze narrowing as he tugged on his hat and watched Dino a little more.

God, it was like looking into a mirror.

Anyone could just look at that child and *know* he was Dino's son.

"Junior for the J. Dino for the D." Karen smiled, the sight honest and true. "You said I couldn't give him the names, not that

I couldn't be smart about it. Most people just call him by the name on his birth certificate."

"JD."

"But I call him Junior," Karen continued, "and he answers to both."

Huh.

Dino's chest felt a little tighter, and warmer.

"But he has no father on his birth certificate," she told him, "and his last name matches his mother's."

Dino could hear the sadness in Karen's voice as she admitted those facts. He absolutely understood why she was heartbroken over doing that, but she had to know ...

"It's safer this way," Dino said. "I'm sorry. Someday—"

"Don't make promises you might not keep, Dino."

Ouch.

She did have a point.

In a way.

"I'm trying," Dino said.

"Trying to do what?"

Dino shook his head, not entirely sure just yet. "I don't know—something, Karen. I just haven't figured out what it is yet, but I do know it's for you and him. For me, too. I just don't know what it is."

"Be happy, Dino."

He blinked. "What?"

Karen leaned up, staring him straight in the eye and leaning forward enough to press a quick and fleeting kiss to his lax lips. "*Be happy.* That's what you should do—whatever makes you happy."

She made him happy.

She had always done that for him.

Dino just didn't know how to keep that happiness without someone like Ben DeLuca coming along to take it from him. It was always taken from him at some point.

"Da."

Dino's gaze broke from Karen's, flying to the boy standing just a foot away. The one-year-old stood in his black lace-up boots, looking like he might topple over at any moment. Still, the baby stood there, staring Dino in the face with a curious expression and his little hand pointing right at him.

"Da," J repeated.

Dino swallowed hard, unsure in his heart.

"I have some pictures," Karen explained. "I showed him—he knows."

"*Da*," J said firmly.

And then he took a step—one hesitant and wobbly, nearly falling over at the same time but managing to get his foot out from under himself to move another step.

His little hands slapped against Dino's knees, and J looked up at him with wide eyes and an even bigger smile.

"Da!"

"Yeah, I'm your dad, little man."

J's smile grew even bigger.

"Well, you didn't miss that, I suppose," Karen said, a hint of a smile in her voice.

"What's that?" Dino asked absently, his attention captured by the smiling child that reminded him of innocence and life.

"His first steps. And he walked for you—imagine that."

CHAPTER 11

Karen

"HE wants you to pick him up."

Dino looked like Karen's statement was the scariest thing he had ever heard. "What?"

She waved at Junior who was looking to his father with hands outstretched, making constant grabbing motions. It was his non-verbal way of asking to be picked up. "He wants you to pick—"

"I don't know how to do that, Karen."

Her brow furrowed. "You just pick him up, and he'll sit in your lap."

Dino still seemed uneasy as he shook his head. "I've never held a baby before and—"

Before he could protest more, Karen leaned down, scooped up the waiting baby, and put him straight into his father's lap. Dino's arms instinctively circled around Junior, holding him tight and close.

"See, nothing to it," Karen murmured.

Her words were bravado and little else. She could plainly see the concern and uncertainty reflecting in Dino's gaze. She didn't think in all the time they had spent together that she could bring forth one memory where he looked as terrified as he did right then, with his own son in his arms.

Not even the day he'd been beaten in a back alley.

Not the times she watched him in court on the television.

Not even when he approached her earlier.

It was a genuine fear—*terror*, even—coloring his eyes. Like he had no fucking clue what to do next, or how to handle what was already in his arms.

Karen thought it was probably far more than just holding Junior. It was likely the whole child and father thing, something she knew Dino didn't have good experiences with. His own father was dead, and the man he had been stuck with after his father's death had been an abusive prick, to say the least.

"It's easy," Karen said softly, reaching out to stroke her son's cheek.

Dino cleared his throat, still as stiff as a board but smiling slightly. "What is?"

"Loving him. Caring for him. Wanting the best for him. *Being* the best you can be for him. It's easy to do those things, Dino. Being his parent is the easiest thing I have ever done. He makes it easy, okay? Don't be nervous."

"I don't know how."

"It's like breathing."

Dino looked over at her, and a recognition lit up his usually cold gaze. "Sort of like how loving you is as easy as breathing."

Karen could and would not deny how much she liked hearing that. But she had other things to deal with before she could really sit down and deal with her feelings about their situation and how she felt for Dino.

More important things were waiting.

Like their son.

"Like that," Karen agreed quietly. "All he wants is to be loved, and he loves you in return. That's pretty easy, don't you think?"

Dino nodded once. "Sounds easy."

"So why are you still sitting there like a block of ice?"

"I'm not sure I'll be a good father," Dino admitted.

Those words broke her heart. For him, and the lack of worth he must have felt for himself and his ability to love. She supposed being treated like trash—like waste, needing to be put out with the rest of the garbage—would leave anyone with a shitty sense of self-worth.

And her heart hurt for her son.

For his excitement at recognizing the man she called "Dad" every time she brought out the photo album on the bookcase. For his innocent love that he wanted to be returned. For the time he had already missed with a man he looked and acted like in every possibly way.

Karen tried not to show it.

For both of them.

"That's not really for you to decide," Karen said.

"Pardon?"

"You don't get to decide if you're good enough for him—if you're worthless or amazing as a father."

Dino fixed the baby's hat, carefully balancing him on his lap at the same time. "I don't understand."

"You don't get to decide," she repeated simply, "he does. The only thing you can do is influence him in one way or the other by the things you do and the way you love him. He gets the final say, Dino."

"Oh."

One little word.

All it took was that one little word for Karen to know Dino would do just fine.

"This is a nice place," Dino said. "Bigger than your last apartment."

Karen found him leaning in the kitchen entryway of her apartment, surveying the space with an appreciative eye. "Not as nice as that house you tried to shove on me, though, right? And I needed a bigger space for all the stuff that comes along with a new baby."

Dino didn't miss her dig about the house if his smirk was any indication. "I was trying to do something right, Karen."

"The thought was nice."

"But?"

"But I didn't feel right taking it," she admitted.

"Yet, you took the lake property."

"You didn't give me much of a choice there, either."

"You could have said no," he pointed out.

"You knew I wouldn't."

"I *hoped* you wouldn't. Big difference."

Karen sighed, tossing the potato into the colander and setting the knife aside. "Say what you want to say."

Dino crossed his arms, never once taking his gaze off of her. In the living room, she could hear the sounds of Junior rolling around in his walker and bumping into things, followed by his babyish giggles every time he hit something. It was his favorite game to play. Karen had learned early on to pack away anything that might break when Junior was let loose.

"You haven't moved into the lake property, either," Dino finally said.

Ah.

There it was.

"I have a job, and it's a bit of a drive from there to the studio, Dino," she explained. "That's all."

"Not that I gave it to you."

Karen shook her head. "Not that at all."

"Okay."

She eyed him curiously. "Why haven't you mentioned the other house? It's closer—it'd be an argument for you to use to get me living there."

Dino's expression blanked, growing cold and emotionless as he replied, "It's not safe. It probably won't ever be, now."

"Mike seemed pretty—"

"Mike is dead because of that house," Dino interrupted.

Karen's heart found her throat. "What?"

"Exactly what I said. His involvement with me beyond a level someone thought was appropriate cost him his life. All because he put forward the paperwork and transferred my money between accounts so I could buy a house. Now, it's watched. It's mine—people know it's mine. I won't put you into it just to have them know about you and J, too."

"You say people like it's just anybody. It's not just anybody, is it?"

Dino didn't even blink. "My uncle is not a nice man."

"Ben DeLuca, you mean. In your letter, you wrote about him a lot."

"He's a monster."

Karen heard what Dino said loud and clear, but she was also listening for what he didn't say. Something she had noted all those months ago when she read his letter—a certain tone he had when he talked about his uncle, and how he referred to himself.

Ben wasn't the only person Dino thought was a monster.

He believed he stared at one every day in the mirror when he looked at himself.

Karen didn't know how to help him to see that wasn't true at all.

"But not a monster I want you worrying about," Dino added when Karen stayed silent. "And that's why I won't push that house on you. It's not important."

Karen fiddled with the sleeve of her shirt, a question burning on the back of her tongue, wanting to come out so badly. She wasn't sure if she should ask. Her heart was screaming at her, wanting to say how she felt, while another part of her wanted to stay safely hidden inside the cocoon of walls she'd built that would keep Dino at arm's length.

Given the way he was staring at her, she knew there was no possible way she would be able to keep him at a distance for long.

Dino wouldn't let her.

Karen really didn't want to, anyway.

There was still a real fear in her heart that made her worry—one day she might wake up, and he'd be gone. To where, she didn't know. How, she couldn't answer.

It was just a possibility.

It happened once.

It could happen again.

"Karen?" Dino asked. "You good?"

She blinked out of her daze, staring up at him and realizing how close he had come to stand in front of her while she was lost to her own thoughts. She could smell the spice and woodsy scent of whatever cologne he was wearing, and she almost wanted to bring him closer, just to see if that smell would swallow her whole and make the rest of the outside world disappear.

Somehow, Karen beat that urge down.

"I'm fine," she eventually said.

"You look a little lost."

Well …

"I am, but it's okay."

Dino cupped her jaw in his large hand, his thumb stroking her skin softly but surely, letting her know with each touch that he understood without needing to be told a thing. "Thank you."

Karen's gaze widened. "For what?"

"Letting me be here. Allowing me to spend time with you and him. Listening to my apology. All of it, really."

"I never planned on doing anything different."

"I wouldn't have blamed you if you had, you know?"

Karen shook her head. "You were right, Dino. All those months ago when you called and said the fact you loved me meant I owed you at least five minutes—you never got those five minutes. I've been waiting all this time just to give them to you."

His thumb stilled. "Yeah?"

"All this time."

"I never told you before, but you're amazing."

Karen's lips curved into a smile. "Come on—save the charm for another day, Dino."

"No charm. I'm leaving us up to you. So, no charm, nothing like that."

"Huh."

"Scout's honor," Dino murmured, winking.

Karen only half believed him.

She didn't mind the charm.

"Let me finish getting dinner ready, and then we can talk some more if you want," she said.

Dino let her go, and she felt the loss instantly, almost wishing she hadn't said a thing, and instead, kept him close. He stepped back, waving at the kitchen sink where the potatoes were still waiting to be peeled and washed.

"Go for it," he told her. "I look forward to a decent meal for the first time in a year and a half."

"Prison food is that bad, huh?"

"Worse. So much worse."

Karen didn't press him for more information, but only because Dino had already turned around and was heading back for the living room. He scooped a small Styrofoam packet—it looked like it was big enough to hold maybe a cheeseburger—off the table. She hadn't asked what was inside of it earlier, but maybe it was something he had been waiting to eat and picked up on his way to visit her and Junior.

"He can have something before dinner, right?" Dino asked over his shoulder.

"Depends on what it is, Dino."

"Something he'll like."

"That tells me nothing."

Dino didn't say anything more, and Karen perked at the sound of her son's squeals when he got his father back in his line of vision again. Already, Karen knew Junior was happy just to be around his father. There was a connection there, and as long as it was fed and nourished, it would only keep growing.

That was pretty amazing.

Junior deserved his father.

Dino deserved his son.

"Dino, what is it?" Karen shouted over her shoulder.

"Just a cupcake."

A *what?*

Why would he get their son a cupcake?

Karen dropped the potato and knife again, heading for the living room. She came to a full stop in the entryway as she saw Dino bend down and open the Styrofoam package, a small chocolate cupcake with rainbow frosting resting inside. On the top, a small candle rested there, and he pulled a lighter from his pocket, lighting the colorful wick.

Then, he held it out to the baby, but not close enough for Junior to grab.

"Blow it out, little man," Dino said softly.

Karen's throat tightened with emotions as she said, "He'll need a bit of help for that."

"Oh." Dino flashed his son a smile, but Junior was far too entranced with the flickering flame on the candle. "Like this, J."

Dino blew the candle out, and Junior's gaze snapped to his father's faze, amazement lighting up his brown eyes. "Da!"

"Happy birthday. Daddy didn't mean to miss it—it won't happen again, I promise."

Karen didn't say a thing about his promises that time.

She needed this one to be one he kept no matter what.

CHAPTER 12

Dino

"STILL just as amazing as it was the first time I saw it," Karen murmured as Dino parked her car.

"It's a little different this time around."

"Oh, how so?"

"Your name is on the deed."

Karen's smile bloomed, but she didn't respond, instead pushing out of the car and rounding to the back passenger seat to grab Junior from his car seat. Dino stayed right where he was in the driver's seat of Karen's car, watching as she made her way up the front steps of the lake house that now belonged to her.

It hadn't taken much prodding on his part at all to get her to come out. She had the weekend off, anyway, and Dino only had to mention how he'd like a day or two with their son before he had to get back to life on the other side of Chicago.

Karen agreed.

Quietly, but she had agreed.

Fumbling with the keys on the front porch, Karen got the front door unlocked and disappeared inside. Dino stayed where he was for a while longer, thinking over what would be happening next, and where he was going to go from here.

Or rather, what he was going to do when he couldn't hide away any longer.

It was a daunting thought, and one he knew would come to fruition a lot quicker than he wanted to admit. Soon, he would make his way back to Chicago, insert himself back into the Outfit and the business, and try to pretend like nothing had happened.

Except something had happened.

Something big.

A much bigger fear rested in his gut, climbing up to his throat and choking him silent. A constant, unrelenting reminder that the things he loved the most—his family, Karen, their son—were not safe in his world.

And how was he supposed to keep them safe, when the largest threat was the person who loved them so much?

Dino didn't have an answer to that question.

Not one that he liked, anyway.

He was selfish, he knew. Selfish because it would be better for him to step away from the innocents in his life that could be stained and harmed by the monsters waiting to jump from his back to theirs. Selfish because he wasn't willing to say goodbye, because his happiness was always so fleeting, and he wasn't ready to let it go.

Selfishness was a DeLuca trait he'd earned fair and square.

But for now …

Karen came to stand at the threshold of the front door, expectantly staring at him from her position. "You coming in or are you just going to sit out there all day?"

He was coming.

Of course, he was.

Opening the car door, Dino stepped out and felt the weight on his shoulders leave for a moment. He could pretend for the weekend that things were perfectly fine—that his life wasn't about to be in shambles again, and that nothing was wrong.

He could have this weekend, surely.

Enjoy his freedom.

Spend time with his son.

Dino found Karen still watching him, her gaze soft and her smile waiting.

Maybe she and him would have a moment or two …

He was going to let her decide that, as he had far too many other things to consider and plan for, and he already knew what he wanted from Karen.

Her.

Him.

Happiness.

Love.

Things that at one time had been so foreign to him, but he now understood the preciousness they held when placed in his hands. As strange as it was, he didn't want to have those things torn from his grasp again, and that really only left Dino with one option.

The only things worth having were worth fighting for.

He'd never fought for anything before.

His siblings' happiness, sure. Their freedom, of course. A position that he never really wanted, yes.

None of those things had ever really been for him. None of those things had ever been something he could hold up and call his own. Dino wanted that—he wanted something that was solely his because he'd earned it, and because he loved it enough to fight for it.

With his arms loaded down with bags, Dino crossed the gravel driveway, stepping up onto the porch where Karen still stood.

"It's a little chilly in there," she said.

Behind her, he could hear Junior smacking something and giggling in that boyishly baby way of his. It didn't take much to make that kid happy, thankfully.

"We'll get a fire going," he told her.

Karen nodded. "You okay?"

"Sure. Why wouldn't I be?"

"You look like something is on your mind."

Dino smiled—something he didn't mind doing around Karen. "Something is always on my mind."

"That could be a dangerous thing, Dino."

She didn't know how right she was.

She would probably never know.

As long as Karen was happy, he didn't think she had to.

This time, he wanted to do it right with her, if she would allow him to. No lies, no hiding, and no games. But that didn't mean he was going to purposely give her information that might hurt her, not if he could help it.

This was just one of those times.

"Let's just have a good weekend," Dino said. "That's the most important thing."

Karen looked up at him as he passed her by in the doorway. "But what about when the weekend comes to an end? You already told me—back to life, right?"

Dino dropped the bags down. "I think I said that wrong."

She didn't look like she believed him. "Do tell."

Junior toddled over to his father on his newly-walking legs, stumbling every so often until his tiny hands grasped onto Dino's pants and held firm. His boy looked up at him with wide, adoring eyes. His son didn't even know him, but he *loved* him.

For nothing more than because his mother wanted him to, because she'd spent time showing him pictures and telling him who Dino was. Karen would never truly understand how appreciative he was for that—how grateful he was in his heart that she cared enough to do that for both him and their son.

"Dino?" Karen asked.

"I'm not getting back to life—I'm handling business so I can have a life."

So we can have a life, he corrected internally.

"What does that even mean?"

Dino reached out to cup Karen's cheek in his palm, and she let him, never moving away from his touch or affection. It was important—a good sign for them, he thought.

"It means you're important, that's all."

Karen didn't ask for another explanation.

"He's out." Dino dropped down on the large leather sectional, exhaustion filling him to the brim. "Does he always fight to sleep like that?"

Karen didn't look up from the magazine in her hands. "Never."

"Ever?"

"Nope."

Dino frowned. "So, it's just me then?"

Karen smiled slightly, amusement lighting up her eyes. "I think it's *for* you, not necessarily about you. New place, his new favorite person, and—"

"Hey, that's not fair."

She did look at him that time. "What?"

Without warning, Dino leaned over and circled Karen's waist with his arms. Holding her in a tight embrace, he pulled her to his side, and with a little urging, she laid her head in his lap. He ran his fingers through the silky strands of her caramel-toned hair, soaking in her presence and life for a brief moment.

"I'm not his favorite person," Dino said. "Pretty sure that's always—will always—be you, huh?"

Karen laughed. "I said his new favorite, not that it was a bad thing."

"I haven't been around enough for him to really—"

"Doesn't matter," she interrupted softly. "You are now."

Yeah, he was starting to get that.

Dino opened his mouth to respond, but the quiet cry from the back bedroom stopped him. Instantly, he moved to go to his son, like instinct beating in his soul, but Karen was on her feet before he was.

"I'll get him down, just relax," she said.

"But I want to."

"He needs to sleep—you make him excited."

Oh.

Well, then, Dino let her go.

Dino turned the TV on, flipping through the channels until he found some action movie that seemed interesting enough to watch. He didn't realize Karen had come back from the rear bedroom until she was standing behind him, and her hand came to rest on his shoulder. Usually, someone approaching Dino from behind would get a bad reaction from him, out of habit and nothing else, but not Karen.

No, he relaxed at her touch.

His contentedness only grew as her fingers traveled from his shoulder to his neck, and then up into his hair. Then, she stopped at the nape of his neck, seemingly content to stay there like she was and touching him.

"Are you going to stay up for a while?" she asked.

Dino shrugged. "I've got a full cup of coffee and a decent movie on."

"Okay."

He heard a lilt in her tone, a small note that caught his attention and made him reach for the remote again to turn the movie down. Glancing up at her over his shoulder, Dino cocked a brow.

"Something wrong, sweetheart?"

Karen smiled. "No. I'm just going to head up to bed."

He wished she wouldn't. He'd rather have her down there with him all night, even if the only thing she did was watch him or look through magazines. He didn't care. Having her close was better than her being away.

It's up to her, Dino. You're letting her make the calls.

Right.

"Sure," Dino said quietly.

Karen's fingers didn't leave his neck. "I thought ..."

Dino was already looking back at the TV. "What?"

"There's only one bedroom downstairs and the loft upstairs. Junior is sleeping."

"I'm good with the couch, no worries."

Except he wasn't.

He'd much rather be in bed with her.

Karen let out a quick breath. "Or you could—"

Dino looked up again, meeting her gaze and quieting her. "Do you want me upstairs with you tonight or not?"

"Well ..."

"You never were shy. Don't start now. Say what you want and I'll give it to you, Karen."

Karen smirked. "Things are different this time around."

"Not that different, sweetheart."

"I was going to make you grovel a little more," she admitted. "Maybe I thought you deserved it after everything."

"But?"

"I don't really want you to."

Fair enough.

Dino clicked the television off, and stood from the couch as he grabbed his full cup of coffee from the side table. He set the cup on the kitchen table as he passed by it, and then rounded the circular stairs, taking them two at a time until he reached the loft.

Karen was only one step behind, never saying a thing, even when they were both facing one another in the loft, stoic and waiting on the other to do *something*.

He'd settled himself on this—they were all up to her.

Whatever she wanted.

Dino was not going to manipulate or sway Karen with his own feelings. If she wanted him back in her life—if she wanted him at all—then she had to make that call, not him.

It had never been up to him to begin with.

"I never really asked you to leave," Karen said quietly.

Dino blinked, taking in those words. "No, I guess you didn't."

"You still left, Dino."

"I'm still sorry, Karen."

Truer words had never been spoken from him before, other than how much he adored and loved her. That was true, too, and it wasn't about to change anytime soon.

"I don't want promises you can't keep," she said.

"Then don't ask me for them."

Karen sucked in a quick breath at that, like it wasn't what she expected, but it didn't seem like she was all that hurt by it, either.

He wanted to give her honesty if he could.

Sometimes it might hurt.

"Okay."

Dino took that statement in, digesting it slowly. "Just okay?"

Karen nodded. "I fell in love with who you were, and for a while, I wondered if that man was someone different, if maybe he was a beautiful lie I'd told myself. I'm only starting to realize that man isn't all that different from the one standing in front of me, I just know a bit more about him, now."

"And?"

"And what?"

Dino pointed at his chest, right over the spot where his heart beat. "And what do you think of this man, Karen?"

"I think he loves me, and he might not be perfect, but he *does* love me."

He did.

Entirely.

CHAPTER 13

Karen

"ARE you just going to stand there after all that and do nothing?" Karen asked.

Dino crossed his arms as amusement colored up his strong features. The hardness of the lines on his face almost seemed to soften when he grinned—not like when he smirked or sneered. This was different.

"I already told you," Dino replied, "I'm leaving us—"

"Up to me. Yes, I got that."

"Then it's up to you, sweetheart."

"Asking you to spend the night *with* me isn't obvious enough that I want you?"

A tic moved in Dino's jaw. "*Want* me, huh?"

A heat coated his tone, making his words feel like a silken caress sliding over her skin. He didn't even have to touch her—he was two feet away—and she still felt like he'd touched every single inch of her.

Karen hid her shiver, but barely. "I do miss you, Dino."

She had barely even gotten the words out before he was closing the distance between them, catching her face in his hands, and then his mouth crashed down on hers. The kiss was bruising—punishing, even as his tongue stroked her bottom lip before his teeth replaced it, nipping sharply into the same spot.

Her whine was swallowed by his chuckle of approval, and as the sound tried to escape, his tongue darted into the heat of her mouth, finding hers and warring there for long enough to take her breath away.

She thought it was very possible that she had missed his kiss most of all.

The way he dragged her closer, how his fingers knotted into her hair to keep her in place, and how her knees damn near buckled under the intensity but he just kept holding her up. He'd never let her fall before.

Those hands—fast and strong—had a goal in mind, it seemed. And that was to get her clothes off as fast as possible. Karen helped, only breaking their kiss long enough to step back and allow him to pull her shirt off. Her pants quickly followed, and as he tugged them down her legs, Dino dropped to his knees at the same time.

She only took a single, quick breath in as Dino's fingers twisted around the waistband of her thong and he glanced up at her, frozen like that for a split second. The glimmer staring back at her, one she hadn't seen in far too long, shined all too brightly.

Lust.

Need.

Want.

God, yeah.

She'd missed this man.

"Breathe," she heard him murmur.

His words were there, the order was clear, but Karen didn't really register what he was trying to tell her. It was only the slightest graze of the tip of his nose along her inner thigh that broke her from the daze.

She realized then that she was trembling, because her body knew what was coming—she knew all too well what was coming— and she didn't want to wait. She *couldn't* wait. It had been far too long.

"Not *too* loud," Dino said, tipping his head to the side, reminding her where they were and the open-concept loft. "But still let me hear it, Karen."

Jesus.

"Anything you want," she replied.

Dino smirked, tipping his face down and nuzzling her thigh again, his mouth coming a little closer to her cotton-covered sex. "Not about me. It's never been about me."

Oh.

Well, then ...

He tugged firmly on her thong, dragging it down over her thighs and to her knees with a slowness that damn near killed her. She was caught like a deer in the damn headlights as she watched him, entranced by how his gaze never once left the path his hands were traveling. Even the coolness of the room, amplified by her nakedness, didn't catch her attention all that much.

Dino was far more interesting, anyway.

Once more, he glanced up at her.

Love.

Promise.

Sin.

She found all of that in the eyes searching hers.

Then he was between her thighs, his mouth encasing her sensitive sex and his tongue flicking out to dive right in between her folds. He didn't give her a chance to think about what he was doing, but rather, ate her pussy like he was a starved man that had just found the most delicious thing he could ever lay his tongue on.

Karen's muscles clenched at the swift, sharp and repeated strikes of his tongue against her already-thrumming clit, which seemed damn near relentless in their intent to get her flying off the edge. She felt his hand slide up the back of her thigh, his fingers dig into her ass, and then his other hand was between her legs, too. The tip of his thumb massaged her clenching entrance, smooth but firm.

Between his tongue and the promise of being filled, Karen found a fast bliss was already starting to race through her bloodstream.

She'd never been very good at getting herself off. She'd spent the last year wrapped up in far too many others things to worry about sex and pleasure.

This was making up for that *entirely*.

Dino's mouth drew away from her body, but not too far. She could still feel the pulse of his breath hitting her exposed sex as he said, "Come on, now, let it go and this gets so much better, sweetheart."

At the same time, that thumb of his was replaced by two fingers driving deep into her wet sex, her fluids smearing along her folds as he opened his digits wide and made her feel so fucking *full*.

And when his mouth was back on her, when his tongue started up that harsh but lovely beat against her clit once more, Karen was gone.

Blissed.

Orgasmic.

Heaven.

Staccato breaths broke free from her chest, and quiet cries clawed their way from her throat. She didn't know how she managed to keep quiet, but she somehow did. And even through the relief of her orgasm, Dino's mouth and his fingers working her body never once stopped. If anything, the rhythm came a little faster and harder, making all those sensations that much better and *sweeter.*

Karen felt the loss of his mouth instantly, though his fingers stayed buried deep in her pussy, massaging against her wall with precise strokes that were only making her even wetter. Dino glanced up, finding her gaze already pinned on him, and with a smirk, he used the thumb on his free hand to wipe across his lips, taking the wetness of her arousal with it.

Then, he sucked it clean.

Her mouth went dry.

"You're killing me here," Karen managed to say.

Dino smiled, and then winked. "Why waste something that tastes like candy?"

Yep.

Killing her.

Karen didn't even mind.

Dino was on his feet in a flash, and kissing her harder than he had earlier before he murmured, "Let me grab my bag."

She knew he was probably going for a condom. After all, it had been her all those months ago that reminded him they weren't always safe and Junior had been a product of that. Despite how much she loved her son, the very moment she had been able and even though she wasn't with someone to need to worry about it, Karen had taken special precautions to ensure there would be no more babies until she was good and ready.

If she ever was …

"It's good," Karen told Dino quickly. "IUD—lasts a few years, so don't worry about it."

Dino watched her for a moment, like he was gauging if her

assurance was enough for him. "If you're sure ..."

"Perfectly sure."

That was apparently enough for him. Dino's arms encircled her waist, and before Karen had even blinked, he lifted her from the floor. Instinctively, her legs wrapped tightly around his hips as he moved them forward, and even when her backside met the freshly-cleaned sheets on the high bed, she didn't let him go. Dino's hands found her legs, his fingers digging in to her skin as he leaned over her, forcing Karen to lean back. His kiss was slower this time, and maybe a little sweeter. The softness radiated over her skin, even as the roughness of his touch kept her very awake and damn near aching.

She worked at the button and zipper on his slacks, pushing them down around his hips before her hands disappeared into his boxer-briefs. Already thick and hot, his cock pulsed in her palm as she stroked him with a firm grip and quick tugs.

Dino's chuckles were a heady sound in her hear. "Ah, fuck, now that's ..."

"Good?"

"Too good, Karen. I don't have the fucking patience for good and slow tonight."

His underlying promise washed over her with wicked intent.

"Good," she echoed.

After all the time she'd waited, she really didn't want good or slow, either.

His fingers ghosted over her jaw as his nose grazed hers and their eyes locked. It was only a split second, one small moment of softness between them, and then it was gone just as fast. His fingers on her thighs dug harder, and he grabbed tight, pulling her to the very edge of the bed. The bed was tall enough that with Dino standing on the floor, his body was angled perfectly against hers.

The position made Karen's breath catch as his cock rubbed along her wet folds. Deep in her very bones, an ache had started to grow, pulsing through her blood with every beat of her heart. It only took a shift of his hips, his hand angling his cock in just the right spot, and he was there.

His mouth met hers as his hips flexed forward. That first thrust, as hard as it came, only took him halfway. She was so wet, her body thrumming with need, but she'd forgotten his girth and it took her a moment to adjust to his size. There was no pain, only the wonderful sensation of being stretched and filled as he worked his way in, his lips peppering kisses over her mouth and jaw while his fingers stroked her skin and his other hand fisted into her hair.

When he was all the way in, that ache only grew from a small ember into a blazing fire.

Dino seemed happy to stay still; Karen couldn't stand it.

"Move," she ordered hoarsely. "I want to be fucked tonight, Dino."

His dark laughter was a balm to her bruised soul.

His second thrust went deeper, if that were possible, the smoothness of his shaft dragging along every single nerve-ending inside her walls. Once his pace had really started—sharp, hard thrusts that made her head fall back and all of her muscles clench with impending relief—Karen found herself giving into the need singing in her body.

He pulled firmer on her hair, the sting making her sigh. His other hand found her throat, his fingers squeezing just hard enough to catch her attention and make her look straight at him.

Love stared back.

Need watched her.

Pleasure waited there in his gaze.

Could they just stay like this for a while?

Could they just stay there, together, forever?

The brutal pace and roughness of his hands were new to Karen. The few lovers she'd had before Dino came into her life and treated her like a china doll in bed—she hadn't minded back then. And even before with Dino, he'd been careful with her, never giving more than she was willing to take from him.

This time, he gave and gave.

Each thrust coming harder.

Each squeeze stinging.

She *liked* it.

That bit of pain only added to the pleasure. And even when it seemed she couldn't catch a proper breath, he was there in her ear, whispering and promising.

Take my cock, sweet girl, and *Breathe for me, Karen.*

He only let go of her throat when his name fell from her lips in a high and broken cry. As airless as the sound had been, it was still far too *loud.* Those fingers he had fucked her with earlier swept over her lips, pressing at the seams with an unspoken question.

She took his fingers into his mouth, sucking the digits in as he fucked her through the second orgasm.

Sweat beaded down her spine.

Her body trembled from her head to her toes.

She didn't even realize she was biting his fingers until his thumb stroked her jaw and she released the bite.

Dino didn't seem to mind all that much.

He didn't say a word, not even when he pulled his cock free from her body, rolled her over to her knees, and filled her full again, fucking her until she felt like she might pass the hell out. He didn't speak until his semen painted her back in hot, ropey streams and their shaking had calmed enough not to rattle the bed.

Karen sighed, happy but tired.

Dino's warm breath washed over her back. "I love you."

She laughed.

"You have a great way of showing it."

She felt his shrug behind her. "Only way I know how."

That was a lie, he showed it in so many other ways, but Karen didn't correct him.

CHAPTER 14

Dino

SLEEP had evaded Dino since his release from prison, or rather, it had for the most part. He'd gotten used to the noise in the cell block from the inmates barking at one another, some singing, and other's doing things he'd rather forget. Even so, the noise had helped to keep him from falling too deep into a slumber where hell might find him. He'd had a few episodes with nightmares while in lockup, but nothing terribly bad.

The very second he had Karen in his bed and tucked into his side, sleep came easily, pulling him under in a tidal wave of exhaustion. The dreams were there, he could feel them edging around the very outside of his senses, but something held them at bay.

Whatever it was, he was grateful.

It was only a strange ringing, a sound he could barely hear in the back of his mind, that brought him awake slowly. Dino blinked, finding the ceiling staring at him as his eyes opened fully, and the unfamiliar loft of the cabin staring back at him.

Karen was still tucked into his side, and seemingly happily so. Her face was hidden against his arm, while her hand was splayed wide to his chest and the sheets had been tugged up just high enough to cover her body. The fabric still molded perfectly to her curves, making his morning erection all the more apparent *and* aching.

Dino ignored it … for the moment.

That ringing was still happening, after all.

Carefully, he pulled away from Karen, not wanting to wake her. It wasn't until his feet hit the cold wood floors did he recognize the buzzing.

Fuck.

Dino headed for the downstairs as quickly, but as quietly, as he could manage, going in search of the bag he'd brought along with a few things he had picked up over the week. He found the bag with the others he'd brought that Karen needed for their stay—J's things, the baby bag, a few non-perishable groceries.

Of course, his bag was at the bottom of the pile. They'd been far too concerned with cleaning up the dust in the place and uncovering the furniture the day before, as well as allowing Junior to explore the inside and outside as much as he wanted. They hadn't put much away, not that they were supposed to stay beyond the weekend, so there wouldn't be much point to unpacking just to pack it right back up.

Dino dug through his bag, and once he had the burner cell phone in his hand, the screen shut off, the call ending. He hadn't recognized the ringing because he'd only picked the phone up shortly after getting his hands on some money from one of the accounts he still had that wasn't frozen, and he hadn't given the number out to too many people.

He hadn't needed to use it, yet.

Still, the number that had been the last caller lit up the screen, and all the anxiety he'd been pushing to the side and pretending didn't exist came racing right back again, full fucking throttle.

Ben.

Dino didn't have any contacts in the phone, he hadn't bothered to input any yet, but he knew that fucking number from anywhere. His uncle had kept the same goddamn number for *years*.

The sad thing was, Dino didn't have to wonder where his uncle had gotten his new cell number from, as he could count on one hand the people he had called after getting out, and that was only for the sake of getting some shit he needed right off hand.

Like access to his banking information to get money.

Theo.

Dino, as much as he wanted to silently curse his brother, knew that he couldn't put too much blame on the younger DeLuca sibling. He hadn't exactly told his brother not to give his number out when he'd contacted him, just that he was looking for a few days of peace before he made his way back to the real world.

Theo had agreed, but at the same time, he hadn't promised much in return.

It was what it was.

The distance between the two brothers had only grown over the last year and a half since Dino's sentencing. Whatever ground they might have been covering to get back to a level playing field with one another was lost after Dino was put away, leaving his younger brother to handle his new position and responsibilities to the DeLuca crew as a mafia Capo.

He never got the chance to tell his brother he was the one who made all that come about for him.

Dino figured it didn't much matter now.

Theo was who he was.

So was Dino.

They just weren't meant to be friends.

Warring with himself on whether or not to call his uncle back, Dino headed for the kitchen to boil water on the stove for a coffee. If anything, it would give him time to think.

Apparently, Ben wasn't of the same mindset.

Not that he had ever been.

The cell phone started ringing on the counter almost the very same second Dino had set it down. He knew better than to ignore the call—one might be forgiven by his uncle, but a second ignored call certainly would not be. Ben was not the type for games, and his superiority complex could not be matched by the men around him.

Especially the men of his family.

What Dino didn't want, no matter what, was for his uncle to come looking for him.

He'd hoped to have some time …

It probably wasn't going to happen.

Dino picked up the call on the second ring, putting it to his ear and stepping outside of the cabin to take the call with as much privacy as he could manage. He didn't need to be waking Junior up before the baby was ready to start his morning, and he didn't want Karen accidentally interrupting his call, either.

"DeLuca here," Dino answered.

"Nice of you to wake up this morning, *nipote*," Ben said drily. *Nephew.*

Ben used that term with affection, for the most part, as though he cared for his nephew as much as he would care for his own flesh and blood sons. Dino knew that was not the case, or hell, maybe it was, and Ben would have been just as terrible, just as abusive and vile, to his own sons as he had been to the nephews he'd raised.

"Uncle," Dino greeted. "Theo give you my number?"

"No, I found it on his desk at the club. Where are you?"

"Relaxing."

"In the city?" Ben asked.

Dino was careful to answer that one, knowing his uncle very well might be looking for him, and not at all wanting Ben to come within fifty feet of Karen or his son. "I'm around, Ben. I needed a couple of days."

"To do *what?*" Ben sighed. "Now, I know you're probably still angry with me over the whole getting you put in jail thing, but deny that it was a good break for you, Dino. You're clear-headed, and you can get back to work doing what is best for the family."

"*The* family, or *our* family?"

"Are we going to waste time playing word games?"

Dino scowled, staring out over the driveway of the cabin and wishing he was still in bed with Karen. "You seem to forget what your little game with me and the police and Feds actually cost me, Ben. I'm on borrowed time, now. They're probably already building the next case—one that'll put me away for a lot longer than a year and a half—as we fucking *speak*. This is not just as simple as a disagreement for us to get over—you practically *shoved* me under the damn bus!"

Without a doubt, and without Ben even needing to say so, Dino knew he had crossed one of his uncle's many invisible lines with that tirade.

But it had needed to be said.

Dino needed to say it.

Ben didn't have to particularly fucking like it.

It took Ben a full minute before he responded, and as he usually was, his response came off as cold and indifferent as his attitude towards Dino had always been in the past. "Be that as it may, *nipote*, you're still free. For however long it is that you'll be out, I suppose. And while you are out, I expect you to do what needs to be done. You're still a made man for the Outfit, after all. You still head the crew, though your brother has been doing one hell of a job on his own, I must say."

"Get to the point, Ben."

"Lunch today, and church tomorrow, Dino."

Dino's gaze narrowed, the cold November wind chilling him to the core as he stood on the cabin's front porch. "What does that have to do with anything?"

"You'll be at my home for lunch today, and in the pew for church tomorrow. Whatever break you think you're on is over—time to get back to life. Otherwise, I have little issue with reminding you of just how easily what bit of freedom you have left can be taken away. Remember, while you have your position in this family, I also have *mine*."

And Ben headed it all, Dino knew.

The most important thing came rushing back to Dino—he had to keep Karen and Junior safe from his uncle, if only because Ben would see them as a threat to him somehow. A threat to the manipulative control he had on his nephew and family; a threat to the suffocating inside world that was their mafia family; a threat to the unhappy cloud of depression and darkness that had followed Dino's life for so long.

Karen had been the light.

Junior was the stars and the moon, now.

Ben wasn't going to take those things away from Dino, and so he would do what he needed to do, for now, to make sure they remained as they were—happy, safe, and entirely unknown to his other life.

"I'll be there," Dino said.

"Wonderful. Bring something for your aunt. She's missed you."

Dino didn't bother to call bullshit on that lie, but that was only because Ben had hung up the phone and not given him much of a choice except to stay silent. He cursed silently, clenching the dead phone in his fist at his side, knowing he didn't get any options here.

Karen wouldn't be pleased that he would need to cut his side of the trip short, but he still wanted her to enjoy the weekend away from the hustle and bustle of the city.

Maybe it made him a coward to do it, but he called a cab before he reentered the cabin, giving the address to the property outside of the city, even knowing it would cost him an arm and a leg to get him back.

But once he was back inside the cabin and upstairs in the loft where Karen was still sleeping her morning away, Dino couldn't find it in himself to wake her. The guilt was a killer, and he battled over waking her up to give some kind of explanation, but he beat off the urge.

Instead, he settled for tracing the curve of her shoulder with his fingers, feeling the silkiness of her skin, and then bending down to press a quick kiss to her temple. In her sleep, she smiled softly.

That was enough for him.

Downstairs, Dino grabbed a notepad and pen from Karen's bag, scribbling off something quick for her.

I'm sorry. Don't be angry. I'll call soon. Something came up.

I love you. —Dino

It would have to be enough, even if it wasn't what she would want.

Until he had something more concrete in his plans, Dino didn't know what else to say. His whole life had just been moving from point A to point B without any real direction or reason, but now that he had *reason*, he still didn't have much direction.

Things were still up in the air for him—and even for Karen and his son—where he was concerned. How long would he be free before the previously dropped charges were refiled and he once again found himself in the midst of a trial, and even lockup?

Was it fair of him to drag her though all that, simply because he was selfish and not ready to let go?

Dino knew the answer to his own question, but he wasn't quite ready to answer it yet.

He grabbed the few things he had brought along and shoved them into his bag as he waited out the cab that had given him a half hour to forty-five minutes wait time. His white Bentley would be waiting for him in a storage locker, thanks to his brother putting it away for him while he was in prison. It wouldn't take long for him to grab the keys to the locker and the car before heading over to his uncle's place.

Dino dreaded that meeting.

He dreaded walking back into a life he had never once wanted.

It was only the quiet mumblings from the backroom that broke Dino from his inner thoughts. Not wanting his son to wake his mother, Dino grabbed one of the sippy cups full of milk from the fridge and the diaper bag out of the corner. He found a grinning, drooling Junior standing up in his portable playpen that doubled as a safe bed when needed. The baby smiled even wider at the sight of his father coming into the room—it damn near broke Dino's heart.

"Hey, little man, come here and I'll get you ready."

Junior kicked and babbled on as Dino changed the boy's sleeping outfit to something else, and got him into a clean diaper. He sucked happily on his sippy cup when Dino put him back into the playpen.

Having spent one night at Karen's apartment, albeit on the couch, he found out that Junior would play happily in his bed for a while as long as he was dry, clean, and had some milk.

Still, he sat on the edge of the bed, letting his one-year-old chatter on.

He wanted to be a normal father.

He wanted to spend every morning with his son.

"Da," J cooed, waving his cup high.

Dino smiled. "Yeah, little man. I'm your Da."

Somehow, he was going to have to figure out a way to make all the things he wanted happen for him and Junior—for Karen, too.

Didn't he deserve it?

Couldn't he be happy?

CHAPTER 15

Dino

"YOU should have woken me up," Karen said on the other end of the phone.

Dino could still hear the anger in her tone, despite how hard she tried to hide it from him. "It was early—"

"Not *that* early, Dino."

"I'll make it up to you as soon as I can, but something came up. Junior was good until you woke up, right?"

"He was—nice touch with the T-shirt, by the way."

Dino smiled at the amusement in Karen's voice. He'd given Junior the shirt he'd worn the day before when the baby had cried as Dino tried to leave. For whatever reason, the boy had stopped, snuggled the shirt, and went back to playing with his toys in his portable playpen.

"He didn't want me to go, either," Dino admitted. "I thought it might help."

"It did, but now he won't leave it alone. Everywhere he goes in the house, that thing goes with him."

"I'll give him another when I see him next time."

Karen was quiet for a long moment.

And then, so softly he almost missed it, she asked, "And when will that be, Dino?"

"Soon."

It was the best and most honest answer he could give to her.

"I'll probably hang out here for the rest of the weekend, in case you get a chance to get away from ... whatever," Karen said.

"You know, you could stay there for as long as you like, Karen. It *is* your home, now."

Again, she fell silent.

Dino let her mull over his suggestion as he pulled off the highway, taking an exit that would lead him into DeLuca territory where Ben's home was located. He wasn't looking forward to this dinner, not in the least. He would have much rather stayed with Karen and his boy.

"It's just not feasible right now," Karen finally said. "I have a job, you know this."

"What if it were feasible?" Dino dared to ask.

"It's not, so there's no point in indulging that at all."

For now, he knew.

But there was a lot about him that Karen didn't know. Like the fact he had a few bank accounts with more money than he would ever know what to do with. Some of the money—or rather, some of the accounts—might be frozen over the coming months as the police and Feds worked their next investigation on him, the one they had promised to follow through with as soon as he was released.

Still, there was money that he had that he knew couldn't be touched by them.

Money that had nothing to do with the Outfit, or his businesses.

Despite how his father had spent the last couple of years of his life—turning rat for the officials—he had set things up for his children, just in case. One of those things had been a large inheritance for each DeLuca sibling that had been put in trust until they were of a certain age. Dino had gotten a hold of his, and his sister Lily's, when he was twenty.

He barely touched his, except to move it into an interest-earning account where it had sat for nearly a decade, gaining more and more money each year.

He didn't touch Lily's either, except to allow her to pull small sums from it when she needed. He had control of hers through the instructions that had been left in their father's Will, and when he thought Lily was responsible enough or needed the money for something, he would sign her account over, no questions asked.

"It could be feasible," Dino said quietly. "If you wanted it to be."

"I don't know—"

"I'm not a poor man, Karen."

"Neither am I, though I might not be living in luxury, Dino."

The heat in her tone couldn't be missed.

Dino flinched, knowing he'd probably crossed a line. "Listen, that's not what I meant. But I would like to take care of my son, and you, if you would let me do that. I'm perfectly capable of providing for you both financially."

"And what about when I start getting my door knocked on because people are following paper trails, huh?"

"Do you mean police?"

"Well, what else would I mean?"

Dino laughed, though it came out dry and a little bitter. "Not all of my wealth has come from illegal ventures."

Although, quite a bit of it had.

"If I need help, let me ask for it," Karen said.

Well, he wasn't about to argue with that.

Still …

"And you *will* allow me to provide for J, right?"

"He's your son, Dino. I didn't put the responsibility on you, but I'm not going to refuse you if you want to take it on."

Good enough.

Karen didn't realize it, and Dino wasn't about to explain and start an argument, but in order to provide for his son, that would also include making sure the boy's mother was in a good, stable position in her life.

He'd started that ball rolling with the lake property.

Dino was going to keep letting the ball roll.

All too soon, Ben DeLuca's large three-level home came into view at the very end of the suburban street. All of the homes in the area were large and the inhabitants toted bank accounts big enough to feed five families, not including their own. Every time Dino saw his uncle and aunt's home, his stomach twisted in knots.

He hated that place.

It brought back one too many bad memories for him, things he would rather forget. Especially the garage where he had been beaten on more than one occasion, and once even had to watch his younger brother take a few hits before being shoved into the trunk of a car for trying to help Dino during one of Ben's many *lessons*.

Nothing about the DeLuca home felt like … well, home.

"I have to go," Dino said, though it was the last thing he wanted to do.

Karen sighed. "All right. You still should have woken me up."

She sounded less angry.

He took that as a win.

"What do you want for Christmas?" he asked.

It was a good distraction.

And the holiday was only a month away.

"Nothing," Karen said. "Why?"

"Shouldn't I get you something?"

It was the first year where he would be able to shop for people he actually gave a shit about. Maybe that would make the holiday a little less dull.

"Why would you get me something?"

"Because you're mine," Dino said, confused.

The silence on the other end of the call only lasted for a split second before Karen's sweet laughter echoed through the speaker.

"Yours, huh?"

"Thought I made that clear, Karen."

"You'll be just fine," she replied.

Dino's brow furrowed. "Pardon?"

"You—for Christmas. You being there will be a great gift. Junior was just a newborn last year, and while I doubt he'll remember this Christmas down the road, it'll be perfect just to have you there to see him be excited for presents and Santa."

Dino smiled. "I can do that."

No matter what, he'd make it happen.

"It's good to have you back, Dino," Terrance said from the head of the table.

Even in someone else's house, the boss sat where he could be at the head of the room.

It was only supposed to be a dinner, that was what Ben had said, but it turned out to be more like a welcoming home party—something he would never want for himself.

"Thank you, boss," Dino said quickly, grabbing his glass for a hearty gulp of the burning whiskey. If nothing else, the harsh liquor would give him a reason to stay quiet.

"You've got a lot to catch up on," Terrance noted.

"I held the house down," Theo said three seats down from Dino.

Dino passed his younger brother a glance, but Theo wasn't even looking at him.

No surprise there.

"Dino still outranks you in the family," Ben said from his spot, directly across from Dino's seat. "Don't forget that, Theo. Take a step back and let your brother pick up where he left off, and you can enjoy a bit less responsibility."

Ben had said that statement so flippantly, as though it wouldn't mean much, and Theo should take Dino's return to their mafia family as a gift of sorts. And yet, the look on Theo's face said he felt like it was anything but a gift.

Dino understood that well.

Theo was just starting to gain some traction with his new position—he had control of a crew, something he hadn't been given before. He had likely been making more money, and his new position would have garnered him more respect from the men around him, who he had hated needing to answer to before.

Now, with Dino's return, Theo would have to take a step back.

He'd be answering to Dino once again.

The slight smile on Ben's face as he took in Theo's scowl, said their uncle knew exactly what he'd said, and had meant for it to cause a little friction between the brothers.

God knew there was more than enough of that without Ben adding more to the pile.

"Theo will still have lots to do," Dino said, focusing on his plate to make sure his uncle didn't know he had caught onto his manipulative scheme. "And it'll be easier for me to catch up with him having both hands in the pot now, so to speak."

Theo cleared his throat down the table, his scowl melting away, though no emotion remained. His mask was perfectly in place—the DeLuca brothers had learned that game well. "Sure, Dino."

"We'll see how long that lasts once Dino realizes how much money he has to hand over to you now that you're doing more than sitting in the corner, Theo," Ben said, chuckling.

Theo didn't grace that with a response, and neither did Dino.

Soon, the topic at the dinner changed, moving onto the upcoming holiday and what would be happening for that. An event at the boss's house—a party on Christmas day. A dinner at the DeLucas on Christmas Eve. The Conti family—Riley, heading his family and the Outfit as the front boss—wanted to throw a New Year's bash for everyone.

They were innocent enough topics.

Dino stayed out of it all, mostly.

He didn't care what any of them did for the holidays. He would show up when needed, make face with people and chat if he had to, but he wasn't going to bother to pretend like he was enjoying himself or that he wanted to be there.

He only had one goal for Christmas—one promise to keep.

He intended to do that for Karen.

"I'll be taking Damian Rossi with me to New York," Terrance said.

The change in topic drew in Dino's attention. One, because Damian Rossi was Theo's friend who still owed Dino a debt from years ago, and because the guy was a lower-level associate to the Rossi crew who also did work for the boss directly. And two, because the topic did not seem to please Ben, if the sneer he was sporting was any sort of indication.

Anything that wasn't good for Ben, or that the man didn't like, Dino was inclined to take notice of.

Especially now.

He still remembered how easily his uncle had put him in jail, and the shit show it had caused for Dino. He was still dealing with that mess, biding his time while he waited for the officials to bring a whole new round of charges down on his ass.

He still remembered how emotionless, yet seemingly pleased, his uncle had been as he visited Dino in the jail, gloating over his manipulation, proud he was still able to teach Dino a lesson for rebelling against his wants, even though his nephew was an adult.

His life would never be his own, Dino knew.

Not while Ben DeLuca was alive.

Except now … now Dino had something—people he loved—

that were entirely his own, and had absolutely nothing to do with Ben.

Unless his uncle found out.

Then, he had no doubt Ben would take them away, as he had so many other things. He would never stand for a threat to his control of his family.

Dino couldn't let that happen.

So, yeah, he started listening.

"Damian doesn't need to go with us to New York," Ben said.

"I want him to go," Terrance replied simply.

"For what?"

"To learn, old friend. He could use the education on other factions and families in this life of ours."

Ben scoffed. "Pardon my opinion, but a Rossi doesn't need to learn anything except how to put down a liquor bottle."

A few seats down from Theo, Tommas Rossi picked up his wine glass filled with red wine as though Ben hadn't said a thing. He took a big drink, making sure to place his glass down with enough force to draw Ben's attention.

Then, Tommas smiled coldly. "All Rossis, or just a couple, DeLuca?"

Ben's expression turned hard. "I said what I meant."

"That's enough," the boss muttered.

It seemed like nothing had changed within the Outfit families since Dino had been in lockup. They were still just as hateful and likely just as prone to violence, as they had always been. Dino put that tidbit away, knowing it might benefit him to use it someday.

When everyone sitting at the dinner table hated each other as much as these people did, it wouldn't take a great deal to make them fight against one another. It seemed there was lots to fight about, too.

The boss had a favorite who one of his closest men didn't approve of.

That was certainly something to use.

Dino couldn't help but wonder if pitting these people against each other might someday be his Hail Mary, though he didn't entirely know why. It was just an idea that suddenly stuck into his mind like a needle, poking and poking, but refusing to let go.

Yes, Dino filed all of that away for a rainy day.

He just knew—somehow—he would use it.

But at what cost?

CHAPTER 16

Karen

THERE was something about the holidays—Christmas, specifically—that made Karen joyful. It could have been the cold snow that blanketed everything, making the city of Chicago look bright and beautiful. It could have been the trees and wreaths, lit up with spectacular lights, and the ribbons draped between each and every light pole, reminding everyone who could see them that the festivity never ended in the city.

Christmas music played in every store.

Bells jingled.

The scent of pine and cinnamon hung in the air.

She loved the season because of how happy it made everyone else, and she liked nothing more than soaking in the joy of others.

Even her son seemed thoroughly entranced by the changes the Christmas season brought. Bundled up with a fluffy coat, big hat, and mittens, Junior peered all around with his wide eyes, taking in every detail he could with loud ohs and ahs.

Karen couldn't help but smile at his innocent amazement.

If only she could get him to leave their small tree and the presents underneath it alone when they were at home.

Honestly, she didn't mind.

His curiosity and excitement were cute.

She thought her son would have enjoyed the sight of the dressed-up horse pulling the white sleigh down the street, had he been with her, but given it was a work day, Karen was taking her lunch away from the studio, and Junior was at daycare.

Maybe she could find out about that horse and sleigh another day ...

Karen tugged off her gloves as she walked into the small café, the scent of warm coffee and freshly baked treats drawing her to the waiting server behind the cash. She surveyed what was offered beneath the display glass, settling on cinnamon rolls and coffee. Once she had paid for her items, she took a seat in the corner, getting her laptop set up as she sipped her hot drink.

She had just got the laptop booted up—ready to do some photo editing on her lunch break—as a figure sat down in the chair across from hers at the small table. The man, dressed in a black suit with a heavy wool coat, looked as though he had come from the outside, and hadn't even bothered to get himself something to eat.

Karen couldn't help but notice how there was lots of other *empty* tables in the café, and her table was only meant for two people. With her laptop out, and a half of a bite of cinnamon roll in her mouth, it wasn't as if she looked exactly inviting for company.

"Can I help you?" Karen asked the man.

The man stuck his hand out, offering it to Karen to shake.

She only stared at him, not taking it.

Pulling his hand back slowly, the man smiled, unaffected at her rejection. "Detective Rubins, ma'am. I was wondering if you had a minute or two to talk about an employer."

Karen sat a little straighter in her chair. "The studio—"

"No, not your current employer, a *previous* one."

A lump grew in her throat the longer she sat there. The eyes of the detective, following her every move, made Karen feel as if she were nothing more than a bug under a microscope.

"Which employer would that be and how did you know to find me here?"

Again, the detective smiled. "I went to the studio first—some of your mail from your last employer had been flagged for return to your new workplace. Your boss said I could find you here. If you would rather something else, I could let you have your lunch and we could set up a time to meet at the precinct."

Hell no.

That thought practically screamed inside Karen's mind.

On the outside, however, she stayed silent.

"Which employer?" Karen asked again.

"A Dino DeLuca—he owns the restaurant you worked at before you moved to your new job."

"I'm not very familiar with him, but I do know who you're talking about."

Karen prided herself on not being a liar, and she had definitely never lied to a cop before.

Detective Rubins nodded. "I'm sure you're aware your old employer was arrested and spent time in jail—this is unrelated to that, in a way. A task force has been put together with the FBI and Chicago Police Department, and one of our focuses has been the Chicago Outfit, something your employer was involved in. You happened to have access to the books for the one business when you were working for Dino DeLuca—"

"I made sure the numbers balanced," Karen said honestly. It was the truth, though she wasn't about to offer any sort of information that might get Dino in trouble where the restaurant was concerned. Certainly, not how she had often cooked numbers when Dino had asked her to, in order to hide cash he'd funneled into the business as profits. "I have no idea about anything of that other stuff you just said. I met Dino a few times while I worked for him, and that was it."

The man didn't look like he believed her.

Karen kept her poker face firmly in place.

"That doesn't explain a visitation record in the prison with your name on it attached to Dino when he was an inmate," the man noted.

Still, Karen refused to crack. "I knew there were legal things happening. I wanted to know if there was something I should worry about because of my previous employment. I thought it might impact my ability to find work if I, too, were being investigated for having worked for Dino before, and felt maybe he would have answers for me. He didn't, and in fact, he refused to even talk to me. Which isn't surprising, considering we weren't friends before he was arrested, and I had quit without giving him notice."

"You have answers for everything, Miss."

"Honest answers," Karen replied.

Or that was the story she was telling.

"Well, should you remember anything that might help our—"

"You didn't even tell me what you were looking for," Karen

pointed out, annoyed.

The detective laughed. "Trust me, you would know without me needing to tell. Which makes me think I've probably wasted both of our times here today. But should you remember anything about working for Dino DeLuca that might help our investigation, please give me a call."

He slid a card across the table.

Karen barely spared it a glance. "Thanks."

But she wouldn't be using that card at all.

"By the way," the detective said as he stood, "was there any particular reason why you happened to quit the restaurant around the same time Dino was arrested? Say, perhaps, you noticed things weren't entirely on the up and up with your employer or his business and you decided to cut tail and run?"

Karen cleared her throat, trying not to shift in her chair. "That sounds like an accusation."

"I certainly didn't mean for it to."

She doubted that.

"I quit because something better came along."

Detective Rubin's gaze narrowed slightly. "You didn't start working for your new employer for a couple of months after, correct?"

How did he know that?

Had the police been looking into Karen for a while?

Refusing to let her inner dilemma or concern show, Karen looked the man right in the eye and replied, "I never said it was the studio, did I?"

"That you didn't. Again, should you remember anything …"

"I'll call."

"And if we learn anything new that we think you might be able to help with," the man continued, "you will be seeing me again, Miss Martin."

The detective left the café without a single look back.

Karen made sure to toss that goddamn card in the garbage as she left the café, and she didn't bother going back to work, either. She called in sick, saying something hadn't agreed with her and she would be back tomorrow if all was well in the morning. Thankfully, her boss didn't question her on the sudden call.

She picked Junior up from daycare, no longer appreciating the snow or the festive decorations lining the streets.

Her mind was somewhere else entirely.

The taste of fear hung heavily on the back of her tongue.

It was only when she was back at home, her son was sleeping soundly in his crib, that Karen finally felt like she could take a breath. Not a good one, though. No, that only came *after* she had called Dino.

As was the usual for him, the call went to voicemail. Since his release a little over a month before, he made every attempt to visit her and the baby a few times a week if he could, and he always brought something along for Junior to have when he came.

Karen let him into her bed every time, too.

She wanted something normal with Dino. She needed stability.

And yet, she couldn't bring herself to ask, for fear of how he might respond to her. She didn't want to tell him that she needed more than someone who just came and went, just in case he stopped coming altogether.

That ... *that* would kill her.

So, she took what he gave.

She didn't ask for more.

When Dino's name lit up the screen of her phone, signaling he was finally calling her back twenty minutes after she had called him, Karen took a huge breath in that didn't hurt.

No, it felt like relief.

And that was every reason why she didn't ask for more.

Even getting as little as she did from him, he was still giving her something.

Something that felt like home.

More could wait.

For now.

Dino arrived at Karen's apartment less than an hour after hanging up the phone. He didn't even knock, just used the spare key she had given him to get in, shrugged his coat off, and found her in the living room. She had found a comfortable spot sitting in front of the bay window beside the lit up Christmas tree, watching snow fall outside on the walkway in front of the apartment building.

"I didn't see you park," Karen said.

Dino came to stand in front of her, kneeling down and placing his hands on her thighs. For a long moment, he stayed like that, touching her softly and being silent as he did so. It was enough to ground the anxiety that had been rushing her nerves like a tidal wave for the last hour.

"I parked a couple blocks away and came in the back," Dino explained. "Just to be safe—seems you're on someone's radar, now."

Karen frowned. "Am I?"

"You did say it was a detective, right? Not an agent."

"That's what he said."

Dino's expression gave nothing away. "Okay, tell me everything that happened. Don't leave anything out, huh?"

Karen did as he wanted, going over the strange encounter with the detective and how it had seemed as though it came right out of the blue. Dino waited her explanation out, never speaking until she was finally done.

"You haven't been approached at all before this?" he asked.

"No."

"And no one around you has mentioned that someone might be asking about you?"

"No," Karen repeated dully.

Dino sighed, standing. "Then it might be just what the detective said. They're looking into my businesses, the restaurant happened to be one of them, and you were an employee on their list to talk to. Nothing to worry about."

He'd said that so flippantly, and she knew he had probably meant to calm whatever fears she was feeling, but it didn't help.

Something just didn't feel right.

"But what if—"

Dino quieted Karen's statement by leaning down and pressing a soft kiss to her mouth. When he finally pulled away, his thumb stroked her cheek gently, reassuring her silently. "This isn't about you—it's about me. I haven't had any officials come my way since my release, but I knew it was only a matter of time. This tells me they are building something against me, or maybe they're getting everything ready before they do come my way. Either way, I know now."

"And what about me?" Karen asked, looking up at him. "Or J, Dino. What about us?"

He stilled, turning into a cold statue right in front of her eyes.

Karen had the distinct feeling that Dino had not given them much thought, but maybe he hadn't meant for it to be that way. He considered his legal troubles as his, for him to deal with alone, but he forgot to factor in that they were still a part of his picture, too.

"I don't want to be left alone again," Karen said softly.

Dino was kneeling down in front of her again in a flash. "You won't, I promise."

"Don't make—"

"I'll make this one and mean it, Karen. Whatever it takes, I will make it happen, I promise. I know it probably seems like you're some dirty secret of mine that I keep hidden away, but you're not. You're so far from that—you and that baby are everything to me. I'm sorry that I can't tell you more sometimes or give you more, but someday I will. I just don't know when or how yet. What is more important is that I keep doing whatever you need to make you happy."

"I am."

"But you could be happier."

Karen didn't deny it. "I don't want to be alone."

She didn't want to be heartbroken at the end of whatever this was. She didn't want to wake up one morning to find out Dino was going to be taken away from her again. She didn't want to be afraid and alone.

She hated how nothing had really happened except for a stupid fucking reminder.

A reminder from a detective that nothing was as it should be.

"Ruined my whole day," Karen mumbled to herself.

Dino chuckled, a small smile splitting his lips. "Maybe I can make it up to you. I can afford to take a night away—I was at the house alone, anyway."

"It's a pretty big house to be alone in, isn't it?"

"It's cold and quiet," he admitted. "I like being here a lot more."

"Stay tonight?"

Dino's arms circled Karen's waist and pulled her from the chair before sitting back down and holding her tight in his lap. His chin rested on her shoulder, and Karen relaxed in his hold.

"Yeah, I'll stay."

She hadn't expected anything different.

CHAPTER 17

Dino

CHRISTMAS, Dino had learned, was a carefully planned event on his part. On the eve of the big day, he juggled his time between dinners and making sure he was where he was supposed to be, no questions asked. After all, he didn't want to be questioned on Christmas when he didn't show up somewhere else.

He could easily say he had been there the day before, and wouldn't be bothered further on it.

The busyness of the season, and the very fact he had been trying to play catch up every single day since his release with business and his responsibilities as a Capo to the Outfit, meant he hadn't gotten very much free time to shop as he had wanted to for presents for his son.

He took a couple of extra hours he had on Christmas Eve to join the last minute shoppers in the mall and small boutiques, and found it wasn't a fun place to be. Claustrophobic and suffocating, yes, but certainly not fun.

But with the presents safely stored in the backseat of his car, and wrapped up beautifully, thanks to the gift-wrapping centers in the store, Dino was satisfied he had done his job.

So when Christmas morning rolled around, the anxiety he had been feeling leading up to the day seemed to drift away. He got up earlier than he normally would; he wanted to be at Karen's place before Junior woke up, and sometimes the kid cracked his eyes open at the first sight of the sun rising in his bedroom windows.

The sky was still dark when Dino pulled into Karen's place. He parked in a lot directly across from her building, one that was meant for another apartment complex, and gathered up the presents in a large sack he had brought along, and entered through the back of the building.

Even though the officials had yet to approach him, Dino couldn't be too careful.

He didn't want Karen to be connected to him on a personal level. The professional connection was more than enough to get her in trouble if the wrong thing was found, or if someone happened to say the wrong thing.

Yeah, careful.

Thankfully, the apartment was still dark and quiet when Dino let himself in. Karen had decorated the place with all the trimmings of Christmas, and the sight made him smile. He'd seen it before now, but with the rooms dark except for the brightly twinkling Christmas lights and the sparkling ornaments, he saw it with new eyes.

It was such a stark contrast to his own house.

One he hadn't bothered to decorate. A place he had only started to fill the rooms with furniture because his uncle felt the need to point out how empty it was and how uninviting it seemed to be.

Dino lived there, sure.

But he didn't want to *be* there.

And therein was the difference.

He didn't even have a Christmas tree at his own house, not wanting to be bothered with the time he would need to take to get one, set it up, buy decorations, and then trim the tree.

It all seemed like a waste, really.

He didn't have anyone to bring over to share it with.

Someday, he wanted to fill that big house with the sounds of little feet. He wanted handprints on the windows, and to stuff the halls with all sorts of decorations during the holidays. He wanted shouts to echo, for toys to be strewn, and for a warmth to spread throughout the rooms that couldn't quite be duplicated with manmade heat.

It didn't seem to matter how high he turned the heat on.

The place the always fucking cold.

Dino knew a lot of that was a figment of his own unhappiness when he was there. His loneliness manifested itself in the strangest of ways, making him feel even more swallowed by the white walls and wood floors of the large house.

That, in a nutshell, was the problem.

The house was just a house.

He had yet to make it a *home*.

Someday, he told himself, *soon*.

Dino quickly dropped the sack of presents in front of the Christmas tree, making sure to carefully set all the gifts in with the ones Karen had already wrapped. He thought he heard the creak of a floorboard coming from the back bedrooms, but he continued his work, adding a few chocolates to J's Christmas sock hanging from the windowsill.

It was only after he had finished, and when he went toward the kitchen to make a coffee, did he hear the shower turn on down the hall. Apparently, he hadn't been imagining things.

Karen had woken up, she just hadn't heard him.

Dino filled up the electric kettle, turned it on, and then went in search of his lover. She had left the bathroom door cracked open a couple of inches—she liked to be able to hear Junior if he woke up before she had finished with her morning routine.

Pushing the door open a little more, Dino found Karen had already stepped inside the shower and the curtain had been pulled closed, keeping her from view.

But the soft humming … low and sweet … made Dino smile.

Karen didn't sing in the shower.

No, she hummed.

She had always called him strange, but to him, Karen was one of the most beautifully different creatures to have ever crossed his path. It was the little things—like her humming melodies in the shower—that he liked the most.

He didn't have a particularly good reason why, he just did.

Dino pulled the door almost closed again, the same way Karen had left it, and went back to the kitchen. He wasn't a particularly good cook, which was strange considering his Italian mother, but he did okay when he was left to his own devices.

And breakfast would always be his thing.

Maybe because it was his favorite meal of the day. Dino wasn't sure, but he went to work, pulling items from the fridge and cupboards to whip up something quick enough to have it ready for when Karen was out of the shower.

He had just slid the omelets onto plates to let them cool when Karen peeked her head around the corner of the kitchen entryway. Her wet hair hung in rivulets around her shoulders, and she hadn't dressed. Instead, her hand clung to a towel wrapped around her body, keeping it in place.

She smiled widely at the sight of him in her kitchen.

"I thought I heard something out here," she said.

"I was here when you woke up."

Karen's head tipped to the side. "Why didn't you come tell me?"

"You're a bear in the morning."

That was a lie.

She was as sweet as sugar in the mornings.

Karen gave him a mock glare. "I'll remember that."

Dino chuckled. "I'm kidding. I thought you might want an easy morning, since J will have you running and cleaning for the majority of the day."

"Oh."

Her soft exclamation made him shoot a smile over his shoulder. He quickly went back to pouring coffee into mugs. It was only when Karen's hand stroked his shoulder did he turn around to face her again.

Sweetly, she leaned up on her tiptoes and kissed him.

"Morning," Dino said against her lips.

"It's a good morning if you're here."

"You did want me for Christmas."

"I did," she echoed, her smile sensual and true. "Are you staying all day?"

At that, Dino frowned, but then wiped it away as quickly as he could. "Not all day. I have a dinner to be at around four."

He could see in her eyes that she wanted to ask him about the dinner, or maybe even why it was important. He was grateful when she didn't, and instead, kissed him again. The second kiss was a little harder—hotter—when her tongue struck out against the seam of his mouth, her demand for him to open up and give her more. They stayed like that for minutes, his arms wrapped around her trim waist, keeping her close, as he explored the familiar heat and taste of her mouth.

The longer they stayed like that, the less Dino found he cared about the food he had made for them to eat before their son woke up. And when Karen's teeth nipped into his bottom lip, and then a little harder on his jawline, Dino found he didn't care to eat food at all right then.

It only took a little shift of his arm at her waist and a quick tug with his free hand, and he had pulled the towel from her grasp, letting the fluffy red material fall to the ground. Dino lifted Karen from the floor with ease, spun them both around, and sat her down on the edge of the counter.

Her breathless laugh echoed in his ear—the heat and want coming out loud and clear as she stroked her hands down his T-shirt and fumbled with the buttons on his slacks. Her legs widened for him, spreading open to expose the sliver of her pink, wet sex between her thighs. He grabbed her legs in a tight grasp, fitting them around his hips as he yanked her a little closer to the edge.

"Bedroom is right down the hall," Karen whispered against his cheek.

Her words said one thing, but her hands were doing something else entirely. He paid no mind to her words, instead focusing on her hands undoing his pants and pushing them down around his hips. Then, as quick as a flash, her warm palm had slipped under his boxer-briefs and circled his cock tightly, tugging with firm, insistent strokes that had his breath catching and his control slipping.

"Fuck, just like that," Dino encouraged, peppering kissed from the shell of her ear down to the corner of her mouth. "Love your hands on my cock."

Karen gripped his length firmer, damn near making his knees buckle. "Let's go down the hall and maybe we can get your cock in my mouth, too."

Oh, he wanted that.

He so wanted that.

"This is good," Dino managed to grunt out.

He wasn't going anywhere until he was buried as deep into her pussy as he could possibly be, and fucking his way to oblivion. She could suck his cock another time—she could make him see heaven another day.

Right then, he just wanted to fuck.

"Get your hand on your pussy, and rub that clit of yours until you come all over my cock," Dino said, pulling Karen's hand from his cock. "Show me how you like it, sweetheart."

The prettiest pink color washed over Karen's cheeks and even down her neck and chest. Still, she did as he wanted, her fingers sliding between her folds, drawing her own wetness from her slit to her clit again and again until she was satisfied. As she started circling her clit with the pad of her fingers, Dino grabbed her jaw, pressed a quick kiss to her mouth, and then tipped her head down.

"Watch me fuck you."

Karen swallowed audibly, but her gaze didn't move from the head of his cock pressing into her sex. One good, hard thrust, and he was home. Surrounded by a sensation that could only be described as crushed, wet velvet wrapping his length like a fist-tight glove.

He didn't really need to think when he fucked Karen.

He didn't need to worry.

He didn't even need to breathe.

No, he just needed to feel.

Dino probably liked that the most—she took away all the shit muddling up his mind, and he only really had to focus on him and her, on getting them to that blissful place where her cries bounced off the walls and heat danced up his spine.

He watched their bodies connecting, too, how his cock disappeared into her sex, and came right back out soaking wet with her and the pulse in the veins. Her thighs shook around him, yet her fingers never stuttered.

"*God.*"

Her word came out damn near airless, so broken, and barely even there at all. He still heard it, and the rhythmic clenching of her inner walls around his shaft as he fucked her harder had his own pressure building in the base of his spine.

The lightest sheen of sweat on Karen's cheeks and the way her bottom lip trembled were the sexiest sights.

Best Christmas morning ever, he decided.

"Okay, are you ready?" Dino heard Karen ask Junior.

"Ma!"

Dino sat back on the couch, enjoying his lukewarm cup of coffee and not finding a single reason worth complaining that he hadn't been able to drink it hot. This was just fine, too.

"Go!" Karen urged, laughing.

Turning his head slightly, Dino listened as tiny feet padded down the hallway from the baby's bedroom all the way to the living room. Junior's eyes lit up and widened as he came to the entryway and took in all the lights of the tree and the sparkling wrapping paper of the gifts underneath.

Then, as quick as the presents had caught his attention, Junior looked to something else, or rather, *someone* else.

"Da!" the baby cried, his little hands shooting out toward Dino as he lurched toward his father. "Da!"

Dino's lukewarm coffee was forgotten instantly, set aside to the coffee table as he stood to go to his son. No matter what, when that kid wanted him, Dino was going to go.

He'd settled himself on that long ago.

Junior bounced happily in his father's arms as Karen came up behind them, a camera already in her hands. She took pictures, and Dino got his boy interested in the gifts under the tree again.

He understood then why he couldn't make his house feel like a proper home. After all, his home was where his heart was, and his heart was with the people who made it beat.

CHAPTER 18

Dino

NOPE, absolutely *nothing* had changed in the Outfit.

The New Year's bash Riley Conti had put together for the four families was a perfect example of just how little things had changed within the ranks. The people were still excessive, still greedier than most, and still liked to show it off.

Dino had to wonder if the rivalry between the families would ever wane, but he seriously doubted it would, unless something serious happened to force them all to work together. It amused him to no end that the older generation of Outfit people had grown up essentially hating one another while playing nice at the dinner table for the sake of appearances.

Yet, the younger generation, the children of those same people, had forged friendships that went much deeper than what it looked like on the outside.

Theo and Damian were a good example of that.

Even Dino's own sister, Lily, and her friendship with Riley Conti's daughter, Evelina, was a bright contrast to the absolute hatred Dino held inside for the Outfit's front boss.

There were more examples he could use, but he didn't know what good it would do these people. Probably very little, as their lives inside the Outfit had taught them all one important lesson that was the same, no matter which family you belonged to.

For the betterment of themselves.

For the respect of a name.

For the rise of a family—the family you belonged to, of course.

It never failed to amaze Dino how much these people had in common with one another, and yet they barely managed to throw a party without some sort of issue coming up to ruin it. After all, one family couldn't very well stand for another to look better than them, even if it was something as simple as a holiday celebration.

Dino was sick of it—he didn't want to be here sharing drinks and fake laughs with these people. Karen had invited him over to share a drink with her around midnight, and if he could get away without someone noticing, he fully intended on doing just that.

He would much rather ring in the New Year with someone he adored, rather than people he was forced to put up with.

Maybe—just maybe—Dino was no better than those around him, who he found himself judging in these situations. He too put on a mask, did what was needing done, and pretended like he wanted to be there. He too hated those around him, yet acted as indifferent as the next person when he was forced into conversation with someone he would rather put in the ground.

It was a strange realization.

One he quickly decided to correct by getting the hell out of the Conti home, and away from the Outfit people. He didn't want to be there, anyway, so why should he stay?

Dino didn't think he would be missed.

He had just slipped past the servers in the kitchen, and rounded the entryway to where it lead to the front of the house, when the sound of someone calling his name in a cheerful way made him pause.

"Dino!"

Despite the friendly tone, the familiar voice had Dino's skin crawling almost instantly. For the most part, he had done well since his release to avoid those he thought might be a detriment to his freedom, for whatever reason. Those people included anyone who was even remotely close to his uncle.

People like Walter Artino.

Dino turned on his heel, facing Walter as the man approached. In his beefy hand, the DeLuca Capo held a glass of what looked to be water, but was more likely to be rum. At his side, the man's snake of a son, Dean, stayed all too close to his father.

He didn't trust these particular men.

For good reason.

Both Walter and Dean were a little too close to Dino's uncle for his liking. They had always been prone to doing Ben's bidding whenever he asked them to, including spying on the DeLuca brothers to relay information back, or whatever the need was that Ben had for them.

Neither the father nor the son cared to hide their doings, either.

Dino highly suspected it was because Walter, for one, was gunning for the position Dino currently held in the DeLuca ranks—the head Capo. And at the same time, he fully believed Walter wanted to get his son the *in* to the family—his long awaited button that he didn't deserve for even a minute.

"Walter," Dino greeted drily.

He couldn't even manage an ounce of respect for this man. He figured it was a damn good thing that he ranked higher than Walter, as it afforded him a bit of leg room to move where he wouldn't get in too much trouble for his attitude.

"I haven't seen you since you got out," Walter said. "How was that, anyway?"

Dino's gaze slid between the father, and then to the son. He couldn't help but notice how Dean avoided Dino's stare, and instead, watched the beige wall like it was the most interesting thing in the room.

Something about that kid made Dino uncomfortable, though he couldn't quite put his finger on exactly what it was that he didn't like. Maybe it was Dean's sense of entitlement, something he had picked up from his father. Or perhaps it was the sneaky, down-low way Dean went about doing things when in the presence of others.

It didn't help that around the time he had started looking after Dean and teaching him a bit of the ropes almost two years earlier, some of Dino's paperwork had gone missing. And then, once that ball had started rolling, it'd taken him straight to the jailhouse, and then to the prison for a year and a half.

He had no real proof that it was Dean who had taken the papers for his father—probably under Ben's direction—but he also didn't have a reason *not* to believe it wasn't Dean, either.

That was enough for Dino not to let the idiots in close again.

Fool him once, shame on them.

They wouldn't get the chance to do it again.

No, Dino didn't care for these Artino idiots at all.

"It's prison," Dino said. "How do you think it went?"

Walter chuckled. "My apologies—you're right. Although, it won't be very long before the possibility comes back that you might be looking at a cell for a while longer, huh?"

Dino's back stiffened at that statement.

A lot of people knew he still had legal troubles brewing, and that forced people to keep a distance from him, and for the most part, Dino didn't mind. As it were, he had been born the son of an Outfit Capo turned traitor, and that branded him untrustworthy to most in the mafia. Dino didn't care to play to their politics, he hadn't chosen this life for himself, anyway. He was more than capable of doing his job and making money without the help or trust of others, as it were.

That wasn't his problem at the moment, though.

No, his problem was that no one was quite gutsy enough to point out straight to his face that he might be looking at more time behind bars.

Not like Walter just had.

It didn't sit right with Dino.

"Looking for your comeuppance?" Dino asked the older man.

Walter didn't even blink at Dino's accusation, simply shrugged. "Someone's going to have to look after your shit, right? Theo can't do it all—he's too young for this. I'll happily fill in when the time comes."

Over Dino's dead fucking body.

He might not care too much for the life he lived or the position he had, but his younger brother was not the same. Theo worked hard to get where he was, and he deserved every bit of it that he was given for his time and effort.

Unlike Walter and his fuckup of a son.

"Keep thinking that," Dino told the man. "Have a good holiday."

He didn't bother giving Walter the chance to say anything else, instead turning on his heel and grabbing his blazer off the waiting coat hook. He didn't turn around as he left the house, either, and he was pretty sure the window rattled when he slammed the door shut.

His exit was enough of an answer.

Let them make of it what they wanted to.

Dino didn't care.

The sun was just barely peeking over the horizon when Dino pulled his car into the garage of his new house. He still didn't feel very attached to the place, and that feeling was only exacerbated by the fact he knew it would be empty because he'd left the most important parts of home way across the city.

It was strange, really.

He tried not to dwell on it.

Karen had been excited to see him the night before, earlier than what he had promised to be there. He'd shown up in enough time to help put their son to bed, but he wasn't able to stay long enough that morning to be there for when Junior woke up.

Work never really ended for a Capo.

Dino cut the engine to his Bentley and eyed the cherry-red Stingray parked in the second stall of his garage, curiosity and irritation churning in his gut.

Apparently, Theo had come to visit.

His house wouldn't be empty, after all.

Dino wasn't sure how he felt about that. He'd been hoping for a bit of a quiet time before he had to travel back across the city for tribute to pay the boss his monthly dues, but it seemed that wouldn't be the case if Theo was inside.

He'd given his younger brother the passcodes to the house's security system if he needed to use it for whatever reason, but mostly for emergency situations.

Theo had a hard time understanding what constituted an *emergency*.

Dino found his brother perched on the island in the kitchen, an apple in one hand and Dino's stack of mail in the other. Theo barely passed his brother a glance as Dino entered the kitchen and went for the fridge, instead continuing to flip through the mail, occasionally opening something if it looked interesting enough.

"Pretty sure that's a federal offense," Dino said under his breath as he looked for a beer.

It was too early to be drinking, but he didn't give a shit.

It was also too damn early to get in some kind of emotional argument with his brother, but it always happened whenever Theo showed up.

"Pretty sure you would just keeping adding to the pile until it rotted through your table," Theo replied just as unaffected. "Do you even pay your bills when they come in, or do you just let them sit there until collectors ring your phone off the hook?"

"Online banking. I don't need papers to tell me what the bank already knows."

Theo didn't respond to that.

Dino popped the top off the beer and took a seat at the head of his table. It allowed his back to be at the wall, while at the same time, allowing him to face his brother. He'd purposefully set up the kitchen that way, knowing there might come a time when he would need to break bread in this very room with people he would never turn his back to.

"What are you doing here?" Dino asked.

"I can't visit?"

"Not when you've had your head shoved so far up Ben's ass lately that you can't see anything but shit."

At that, Theo did look to his brother, a hint of anger flashing in his familiar brown gaze. Their eyes were unmistakable—DeLuca eyes, that same brown with gold flecks surrounding the pupil. And when they got angry, that brown damn near turned to a flat black.

"Are we just ignoring the fact you left me hanging in the wind for a whole year and a half without so much as a fucking phone call, then?" Theo asked.

Dino rested back in his chair, never taking his gaze away from his brother. "That's your problem? Your feelings are hurt because I didn't give you a call while I was in lockup?"

Theo's brow furrowed and he glanced away. "I thought ..."

"What?"

"I thought we were getting better before you—you know what, never mind." Theo pushed down from the island, his boots snapping hard against the tile. "It doesn't matter what I thought, Dino."

"You thought we hadn't burned all those bridges after all."

Theo's jaw clenched, but he turned away, hiding the anger. He tossed the remaining pile of mail to the island, apparently done with the conversation and ready to leave. "Like I said, it doesn't matter. Just like when we were kids, you left me out to fucking dry, man. I'll always be filling your spot and walking in the footprints you left behind—we're older now, though, so I just get to do it in a different way."

"You have no idea what you're talking about," Dino replied calmly.

He knew Theo was telling the truth on one part.

No matter what Dino said, Theo would never listen. He would never really hear his brother tell him the truth, because he was too focused on everything else that had been told to him over the years.

His position—his title—and all that work Theo had to do while Dino was in lockup had only been to his benefit. He'd gained a spot that couldn't be taken from him now unless someone killed him for it, and that had only come about *because* Dino made a call for his brother.

"You're going to have to learn things on your own time and at your own speed," Dino said as Theo crossed the kitchen floor, heading for the garage. "I can't fill in all the blanks for you Theo, no one did that for me."

Then, Theo stopped, turning to glance over his shoulder at his brother. "Do you know why I even came here today?"

"To piss me off?"

It wouldn't be unusual or new.

"No," Theo said, practically spitting out the words. "To warn you, though I don't know why I even fucking bother. Where were you on Christmas, Dino?"

Dino straightened in his chair. "Here."

"Bullshit."

"I was here, Theo."

He was sticking to that story, no matter what.

Theo shook his head. "You weren't. Ben wanted to have dinner—he called the house, you didn't answer. He sent me over, you weren't here. I waited, you didn't show. Last night, you left the party, and no one might have noticed, but Walter couldn't keep his fucking mouth shut and bitched to Ben about your little run in. Ben sent me over here today to let you know he wanted to speak to you this morning. Guess what I found *again*?"

Dino hadn't been there when Theo showed up.

He still refused to speak.

"Yeah," Theo said. "But I covered for you then, right, and I'll probably keep my mouth shut today, too. Don't worry about filling in the blanks, brother, I don't care to know."

Dino blinked, unsure of what to say.

"Secrets don't stay secret in this family for long, Dino," Theo continued, still as cold an unaffected as ever. "I don't know what you're hiding, but get better at hiding it before Ben goes looking for whatever it is."

Point taken.

CHAPTER 19

Karen

"BOO," Junior said, pointing to the blue colored square.

"Well done," the pediatrician praised. "Green?"

Easily, Junior pointed to the smaller oval shape on the wall. "Ween."

While he still had a way to go with pronunciation, the boy did exceptionally well with colors, shapes, and recognition. Karen attributed a lot of that to his days spent at daycare where the caregivers worked a lot with the children, but she also had a lot to do with it. She spent her nights reading to her son, as much as he wanted, until he fell asleep, even. He had all sorts of learning games to play, and educational toys to pass the time.

Junior loved to learn. At only fifteen-months-old, the boy was above his age group in learning efforts, and Karen fully planned on keeping him that way. It was much easier to deal with a toddler and their tantrums when understanding them was a possibility. To understand, she needed her son to communicate.

Now, he could do that.

Mostly.

Then, the older gentleman turned to Karen, a smile crinkling his features. "His fine- and gross-motor skills are above par."

Karen couldn't help but be a little proud about that fact. "Oh?"

"He already has a wide vocabulary of words. It's impressive. Try getting him to put words together to form even two- or three-word sentences."

"I will."

She was already trying to do that with Junior, and sometimes he would put two words together if he really wanted something enough.

But almost always, the only thing he would put together to say or ask was, "Momma, Da?"

It was the boy's way of asking his mother where his father was when he wanted Dino, and while Karen never had a good answer for him, Junior didn't really seem dejected when he was given a non-response. If anything, he just waited his father's next visit out.

"If he keeps this up, he'll be beyond his learning curve and probably won't need pre-K at all before starting kindergarten." The pediatrician looked over Junior's chart, humming under his breath. "It's February—his next needles are due at eighteen months. Make sure to have that appointment done before you leave the office."

Karen nodded. "Thank you."

The doctor gave Junior one of his gummy treats before leaving the office and giving Karen one last goodbye. She quickly got her son dressed in his winter clothing, avoiding sticky kisses as she tugged on his large hat to get it on his head.

"Ready?" she asked the boy.

Junior smiled widely, his teeth stained red from the candy. "Go!"

Twenty minutes later, Karen juggled her boy in one arm while trying to unlock her apartment door with the other and keep her three bags of groceries from dropping to the floor. She didn't have to try for very long, because the door swung open, exposing a smiling Dino waiting behind it.

Immediately, J squealed at the sight of his father. "Da! Momma ... Da!"

Karen huffed, shifting her squirming boy to Dino's waiting arms. "Yeah, I see him. A little help getting up the stairs would have been awesome."

"I was in the kitchen, or I would have come to help," Dino said.

Her irritation melted away when Dino easily swapped her bags from her grasp to his, all the while keeping a firm hold on the baby. Then, he gave her a quick kiss.

Karen smiled. "I didn't know you were coming over."

"Last minute thing."

It almost always was.

Karen didn't mind.

"You were in the kitchen—did you cook?" she asked.

Dino smirked a sinful sight. "I only do other things in the kitchen when you're in there with me."

God.

Her cheeks pinked, and Karen quickly moved inside the apartment and closed the door for fear her neighbors might overhear their conversation. She didn't understand how Dino could say something like that with a baby in his arms and still look goddamn attractive, but he managed it.

"Stop that," Karen muttered halfheartedly, tugging off her jacket and mittens. "I just want food."

"Oh, I have that for you, too."

"Great."

Dino unwrapped Junior from his winter clothing as well, setting the boy to the floor as soon as he was done. The very second Junior's sock feet hit the floor, he was off running toward his bedroom, probably in search of his newest toy to share with his father.

It was a game the two played.

Karen sometimes found herself amazed at how Dino could sit with J for hours on end, listening to the boy press the same four buttons on a toy over and over again and seemingly never getting bored.

If nothing else ever mattered between them, she knew he loved his son.

Entirely.

Wholly.

Truly.

He loved that boy more than he loved himself.

"You look cold."

Dino had no sooner said the words before Karen found herself bundled in his embrace. Warm hands covered hers, taking away the chill from her skin. She rested her head on his chest, happy there for the moment. All it took was a press of his lips to the top of her head, and Karen forgot all about the stress of the busy day.

Soon, Dino would probably leave.

Maybe for a couple of days.

Maybe for a week.

She had come to expect that from his visits—one minute he was there, and the next hour he was grabbing his things without much explanation. She knew a different woman—maybe a better woman—wouldn't put up with his transient behavior and the lack of explanation that went along with it.

Karen was not that woman.

She took what he gave, because she loved him just as he was.

She still wanted more sometimes, but she had come to appreciate the amount of time and affection Dino could provide in his passing moments when he was around.

"The pediatrician said he's too smart for his own good," Karen said.

Dino chuckled. "Already knew that."

"You could have let me know you'd be here today."

"Did I have to?"

Karen shrugged. "No. This is good."

"Da!"

The singsong tune followed their son's cry, the *ABCs* belting out from a train-shaped toy Junior had plucked up from the toy aisle at their last trip to the mall.

"Bee, Cee, Dee," the baby sang, plopping down to his bottom at his father's feet. He held the toy high, urging Dino to take it. "Twane, Da."

"Train," Dino corrected, plucking the toy from his boy's hand. "It's very loud, J."

"He always picks the loudest ones," Karen mused.

Dino gave her a wink, and in that split second, her heart melted. "The loudest toys are the best ones."

And these moments were the ones that explained exactly why Karen never complained about Dino, or his constant coming and going from their life. Whatever was happening on the other side of the city, whatever worries had sent him running for a safe haven with them, it didn't really matter.

Not when he picked his son up and fell to his back on the couch, already focused on the toy in his hand and the baby sitting on his middle. They were the most important things to him. He showed it in so many other ways that she knew no one else got to see.

"I didn't actually cook," Dino said absently. "Just grabbed some take-out. It's in the kitchen."

Karen dropped a kiss to his forehead as she passed him by. "Take-out is great."

And so were they.

"No, no, no," Karen said, laughing as Junior squealed as loudly as his little lungs could. "Not today, little man. I am late—you're going to make me go broke buying more toys."

"Toy! *Toy!*"

Karen was starting to feel betrayed by her love of coffee, considering her favorite coffee shop, where she stopped at every morning before dropping her son off at daycare, was situated directly beside a toy shop. Almost every day, the toy shop changed its front display. Today, the large glass showcased a giant wooden train set that filled up the entire space. It must have been electric or battery operated, because the train was moving over the tracks at a slow speed.

"Toy!" Junior shouted again.

"Coffee," Karen replied, grabbing the handle of the café's front door. "Your mom needs coffee to get through the day so I can have more money to buy toys, Junior."

That didn't seem to placate the boy.

She didn't get the chance to open the café door, because someone else came barreling out with their head down, their attention stuck on their phone. She wasn't able to get out of the way in time, and the man slammed right into her, almost knocking her to the ground.

Somehow, she managed to stay upright on the slippery sidewalk, plus keep her son firmly in her arms.

Ready to bitch the distracted guy out, Karen faced the man, but quickly fell silent.

Familiar features stared back at her.

Light brown, almost blond hair. Strong jaw. Brown eyes with flecks of gold.

"Damn, I'm sorry," the guy said quickly, stuffing his phone in his pocket. "You okay?"

She recognized him from somewhere, but it took her a minute to draw *where* exactly her memory was coming from.

Theo.

Theo DeLuca.

Karen had only met him once before—a long time ago, at Dino's club when she had gone there looking for a job and Theo had been the one to vet the girls. They hadn't even really had a decent conversation, but his face was unmistakable.

There were differences, sure, but his features were too similar to his brother's for her not to see them.

Karen's mouth wouldn't work, even though she tried.

Theo blinked, taking Karen in again and she saw the recognition light up in his eyes. Then, just as quickly, his gaze darted between her face, and the baby in her arms. Karen's grasp on her son tightened a bit as Theo's gaze lingered on the baby boy.

"Toy!" Junior said, still pointing back to the shop window where the train was going around the tracks. "Momma, toy!"

"Not today, J," Karen said faintly.

"It's Karen, right?" Theo asked.

Karen straightened a bit, holding her son impossibly closer. She had no reason to be frightened of Theo—he was Dino's brother, after all. She knew a bit about him, and Dino had explained some of what she didn't know.

She was also aware that Theo had seen her more than that one time she had met him at the club—like the time when she had come looking for Dino after he had ignored her. Apparently, Theo had been eavesdropping on their conversation that night.

"Karen," Theo said again.

Her gaze snapped up to his. She decided to feign ignorance, not knowing what else to do. She had the distinct feeling that if Dino meant for her to be around his family, he would have brought her around a long time ago.

"And who are you?" Karen asked.

"Momma!"

Theo's gaze went back to the baby, and the black fabric he held in his hands. Silently, Theo reached out to grab the T-shirt Junior held, looking at the band emblem on the front of it. Junior still took shirts from his father to have as a sort of comfort to use during the periods Dino was gone. It helped to get the boy to sleep, and Karen needed all the help she could get.

Had he seen his brother wearing that shirt the week before?

Would he recognize it?

Just as fast as he'd looked over the shirt, Theo let it go.

"He likes trains?" Theo asked.

"He likes toys," Karen replied quietly.

Theo looked at the baby again, but Junior was more interested in pointing at the window display. Still, Karen knew he was looking at the same damn thing that stared back at her every day when her son was sitting right in front of her.

Familiar eyes.

Familiar features.

Familiar.

"Have a good day, Karen."

She still hadn't confirmed her name to him, but he used it like he just knew.

Karen supposed he probably did.

Theo gave Karen and the baby boy one last glance before he turned away. "Sorry about bumping into you like that."

"It's okay, Theo."

And just like that, Theo smiled, nodding once.

When Karen came out of the café, the owner of the toy store was standing in front of his window display. Once the man saw her, he waved her over.

Apparently, the display would be packed up and ready for her the next day.

"Pardon?" Karen asked the man.

"The boy's uncle—he bought it for him. Said not to tell anyone, it's a secret. I laughed it off, but he seemed pretty serious about it."

Karen understood perfectly well.

Dino didn't tell Theo a thing.

Theo didn't tell Dino a thing.

Because in their life, not knowing was better.

Even if she didn't like it, Karen would have to play along.

CHAPTER 20

Dino

THERE was a change coming; Dino could feel it in his bones. Something was happening outside of his circle of people, something he probably wasn't going to like.

And even if he didn't know some of the things happening, like search warrants being served for some of his businesses, and employees of his being pulled in for questioning, Dino still knew. It was a sensation that had burrowed deep into his bone marrow, as though spikes had been driven into his bones.

Dread, he recognized.

The feeling was dread.

He'd watched the winter leave almost too slowly for his liking, replacing the snow with spring showers and warmer days. Usually, he wouldn't have noticed the seasons changing around him, it was just another season, but he'd started counting the time passing in a different way.

Days he spent with his son and Karen.

Days he didn't see a detective or federal agent waiting outside one of his places.

Days he was still free.

On the outside, Dino was the perfect picture of composure. He didn't show how much it bothered him that officials were digging into his businesses and keeping him from making the money he should be through his more illegal ventures. He didn't bother explaining to the other Capos in the family who were less than willing to work with him because of his increased attention that he'd begun hiding and funneling funds into accounts that couldn't be touched by officials when the time came for them to once again, freeze his accounts.

Outside, he was perfectly fine.

Business went on to the maximum he could work.

He showed his face when needed or asked.

The world kept turning.

But inside?

Inside, Dino was panicking.

Ostracized by a lot of men in the Outfit for fear they too would come under investigation, he used his brother's position to get things done when needed. He didn't tell Karen how close he felt it was to something big happening with the investigations that were currently underway because the very last thing he wanted her to do was worry about him.

It was going to happen.

It was just a matter of *when*.

Dino was so painfully aware of that fact as he sat at his desk, signing paper after paper, getting asset after asset allocated to where he needed them to go. He didn't think of very much else, except his current task.

It was a task he had been working on for months.

If he could help it, Dino wouldn't go to jail. He wasn't going to spend his life behind bars because officials had some kind of hard-on for him, and hoped that at some point, he would turn for them and work for their benefit.

As much as he hated the Outfit, Dino would never turn rat.

He had far too much pride for that.

But it seemed someone had their eye on him—someone was determined that if they couldn't get a leg into the Outfit, then they would start smaller by chipping away at what chunks they could, until it all began to crumble in on itself.

Dino refused to be the starting piece to that puzzle.

And also, he had promised.

He'd promised his son to be there for his birthdays.

He'd promised to be *there*.

Dino was not going to be there from behind bars.

His arrest was inevitable.

The rest was entirely up to him—he just hadn't figured out a plan yet.

Except this part, he thought, opening up the last folder in front of him.

Last Will and Testament, it read.

Carefully, and privately, he'd worked on things like this over the winter and leading into the unusually warm spring. It had taken a while, and with very well-placed steps and calls, he had gotten a particular lawyer in another state but with a license to work in Illinois under his payroll.

Someone who wouldn't be picked up on Ben's radar.

Because yeah, Dino still needed to worry about his bastard of an uncle, too.

He was always on the back of his mind somewhere.

Dino read through the pages of his Will, taking in what he had asked to be done and who should be the one to do it. It was all simple enough, as it should be. He didn't think his death would be on the table, but shit happened.

An unprepared man was one who left behind a mess.

He wasn't preparing to die.

However, he *was* preparing for anything.

Think, Dino.

His internal voice wouldn't shut up lately.

Get your head in the game—plan, plan, plan!

That would be a hell of a lot easier to do once he knew exactly what he was planning for.

"Dinner, tonight?" Karen asked on the other end of the call.

Dino smiled, happy that he could actually say yes. It had been a long week, one that kept him on the other side of Chicago and away from Karen and his son. He knew she was missing him, and fuck if he didn't miss them, too.

"Of course," Dino said. "I have one thing to pick up, and I'll be over."

Actually, he had a racket payment to pick up from a construction company, but he figured the little details were unimportant, and sometimes, the less Karen knew, the better. Plausible deniability, after all.

"Do you want me to grab something?" Dino asked.

"No, I've got—Junior, get off the table right now!"

Somehow, Dino managed to keep himself from laughing. Junior had taken to climbing on things over the last couple of months. The seventeen-month-old toddler kept his mother constantly moving, and the higher he could go, the better.

One morning, Karen told Dino she had come out of the bedroom to find Junior had used the cupboards as stairs to get up onto the counter, and then proceeded to pile things against the fridge so he could climb on top of that, too. He only cried out for his mother to come help him because he couldn't get down.

As amusing as it was, it was also terrifying to Karen.

Dino tried to understand—sympathize, even.

Junior was a boy; he had the DeLuca blood running all through his veins. He was going to climb. He was going to explore. He was going to get himself in all sorts of shit that would turn his mother gray long before her time.

It was just a fact of life.

Still, Dino knew, the boy would be fine. He'd come out of every incident unscathed, much like how his father had, and the men that came before him. It was just their way.

Dino couldn't exactly explain all of that to Karen without pissing her off, so he didn't bother. She would learn, and she would grow to like it—or tolerate it as much as she possibly could.

His mother had.

"I hear you chuckling," Karen muttered to Dino.

He could hear Junior in the background, repeatedly shouting "No" at his mother as she pulled him off the table and set him back to the floor.

"I'm not going to apologize," Dino replied. "Better to let him go—it tires him out."

"Easy for you to say, Dino."

"I speak from experience."

"Whatever," Karen said, laughing but still managing to sound annoyed at the same time. "Say hello to Daddy, J."

If it were possible, Dino's smile grew impossibly wider

"Daddy, hi!"

Over the last few months, J had taken to calling Dino "Daddy" rather than the previous "Da" he had been using. His words were much clearer, mostly thanks to Karen and her constant need to teach the boy. While it made him sad to see some of the babyish expressions leave his son, it also excited him to watch Junior grow into a too-smart-for-his-own-good toddler.

It was a strange thing to feel both sad and happy about the same thing.

Dino supposed that was just a part of being a parent.

Something he had never thought he would be.

"Hey, little man," Dino said, turning the corner at the same time.

His boy chatted away, and from the sound of the rushing noise in the speaker, he was running through the apartment at the same time. A ball of energy—that was how Dino would describe his son if he was ever asked to. The kid never slowed down for anything, except maybe a book and food.

Unfortunately, while his son talked and talked, Dino's attention had been grabbed by something else. Or rather, two people. He would have much rather talked to his son, but he didn't think he was going to be able to as he stared at the waiting men.

Standing next to his white Bentley, two men dressed in dark suits faced him as he approached. He didn't worry much about *who* they were, because with just a single look, he already knew.

Cops. Detectives. Agents.

It didn't matter—they all smelled the fucking same.

One of the two held a folded up piece of paper in his hands.

A warrant?

Probably.

"J?" Dino asked, never turning around as he spoke to his son.

"Yeah, Daddy?"

"I love you, okay? Tell Momma that I'm sorry."

"Why?"

His son's innocent question broke his heart, but Dino didn't know how to truthfully answer it without also killing himself in the process. Karen would figure it out. She was smart like that.

And she was good to him, too.

Too good, even.

She would let him apologize when he was able.

She would forgive him.

Again.

Dino wished he was better at this whole relationship thing—better for her.

He hung up the phone on his son, who was still asking his father questions, though it was the very last thing he wanted to do.

"Dino DeLuca," one of the two men said, stepping away from the car, "we've been waiting for you."

As he came closer, Dino recognized the fools.

The same agents who had arrested him the first time—yeah, someone definitely had a hard-on for him.

"That a warrant for my arrest?" Dino asked, nodding to the paper in the other man's hand.

"Good guess," the agent replied.

Wonderful.

"You don't seem surprised, DeLuca."

"You've been digging through my businesses and questioning anyone I came in contact with for the last year," Dino said. "You've pulled my tax records, any banking documents you could, and even managed to get one of my accounts frozen just last month. Do you think I'm fucking stupid? I knew what was coming."

"Good, then let's make this easy."

Oh, he would.

For him.

Dino dropped his phone twenty feet from where the agents stood, knowing he'd have more than enough time to destroy it before they could get to it. On a rainy street, he crushed the burner phone under the heel of his boot, ruining it entirely.

Karen only called him from a burner phone he had provided to her.

It was just another failsafe.

He was never going back to prison.

But she'd never go there, either.

Not for him.

Tax evasion. Fraud. Money laundering.

Dino read over the charges, the list substantial.

Twenty-five to life.

That's what all it would add up to. He knew it without needing to be told. It was every *Mafioso's* greatest fear. A lot of made men didn't fear being put in prison for something like murder, something at least all of them had committed once in their careers, but rather, the *details*.

After all, the devil was in the details.

No, men like him didn't fear being caught for the bad, *bad* shit.

They feared being caught for the details of their lives—the byproducts of being criminals, making money illegally, and hiding it how they needed to in order to be able to actually fucking use it without questions being asked.

Wiring money between countries. Funneling money into businesses that mostly made profits by cash-only. Lying on tax returns because cheating the government was better than paying taxes on dirty money.

Those were the details that almost always put men like Dino away for life.

The charges racked up one after another.

He read down the list again.

Bang. Bang. Bang.

He could almost hear the prison cell closing on him again; the sounds of the chatting inmates so late at night that his fucking ears rang. He could smell the cinderblock walls and barred windows.

No, he wasn't going back there.

"We can talk about this," the agent said across from him, "all of these charges—"

Nope, he wasn't playing that game, either.

"Get my lawyer."

It was his mantra.

Dino was sticking to it.

151

"You're going to take twenty-five years—probably more—for what?"

Loyalty.

Honor.

Respect.

He'd take it for a lot of things because that was just what made men did.

Except he wasn't going to take it at all because he had his whole life waiting for him across the city. It had just taken him a long damn time to find her.

"I'll wait in a holding cell until my lawyer gets here," Dino said.

The agent scowled.

That was that.

CHAPTER 21

Karen

THE soft knock on the studio door had Karen turning away from the toddler dressed up in her very best dress. The girl's mother went to distract the child as Karen asked for a minute of privacy, and excused herself from the room.

Her boss waited as Karen put her camera safely away and came out to join her in the hallway. Unfortunately, the woman wasn't wearing her usual smile. It was the first obvious sign that something wasn't right.

"What's up?" Karen asked. "Something wrong?"

She liked her job, for the most part. Photography was her thing—she took a great deal of pride in it. She didn't get to freelance as much as she used to, but frankly, it didn't make her as much money as the standard family shoots that the studio provided did.

She was still holding a camera, though.

She was still taking pictures.

Karen figured that was the most important part.

"I don't know, maybe you could tell me if there's something wrong," her boss said.

Karen's brow furrowed. "I'm not sure what you mean. I've been working this session for a half an hour now. The mother wanted the nature backdrops."

"No, not that. You have a visitor." Then, her boss frowned, her voice lowering as she added, "If you're in some kind of trouble,

Karen, I need to know."

What?

The confusion on her face must have been enough of an answer for her boss, because the woman only nodded.

"I'll finish the session—the detective is waiting in the main room."

Oh, fuck.

Somehow, Karen managed to keep her composure, but barely. As her boss said, the detective—the same one that had approached her months earlier—was sitting on the leather couch, sipping from a cup of to-go coffee.

She didn't bother to sit beside the guy.

"Detective Rubins, right?" Karen asked.

The detective nodded, smiling as he set his cup down. "Sorry to bother you at work, Miss Martin."

"Are you? Because with no context, my boss seems to think she had to worry about employing me. If your goal is to pressure me into something, this is not the best way to go about that, I assure you."

"No, of course not. Sit, I want to chat for a moment. I have some developments I've been asked to share with those who might be able to help our investigation, even if it is by proxy."

Karen still didn't sit. "I thought I made my position clear the last time?"

"You—"

"Didn't know Dino DeLuca well, I worked for him at a restaurant to keep his books managed, and quit when I found something better."

The detective nodded, letting her finish completely before he spoke again. "That's all true, and from what we *know*, it's also accurate. But we have reason to believe you, like a few other of Dino DeLuca's previous and current employees, possibly have more information to share or help explain certain things, but you likely need a safe way to do so. Seems a great deal of people around Mr. DeLuca know of his involvement with a criminal organization here in Chicago, and that sometimes leads people to think speaking up wouldn't be a safe option."

"Is there a point here that I'm missing?" Karen asked quietly.

"We arrested Dino yesterday."

Karen's heart broke all over again.

She had already known because when Dino hadn't shown up for supper, she'd gone looking for any sort of explanation as to why. Calling his phone hadn't worked. But a quick check of the local news told her an arrest had happened involving an Outfit figure, and more information was to come.

It didn't take a genius to figure it out.

Karen wasn't fucking stupid.

"Again, the point?" Karen asked.

How she managed to keep her tone calm, Karen didn't know.

"Our case is solid, for the most part," the detective explained, "but we have areas we would like a better footing on. We've been going back over our list of people we questioned previously, and you happened to be on there. We're hoping that some people might feel more comfortable coming forward now that one of the major issues has been taken off the table, or rather, off the streets."

Taken off the streets.

Karen swore she could taste bile on the back of her tongue.

This man—this detective—was just doing his job. She understood that all too well. But what he didn't know, and what she could never properly explain to him, was that the same issue he had removed was the very person Karen loved. Someone her son adored with his entire little being. She might have made up the heart in her small world of people she cared for, but Dino was the soul to it.

She could live without a soul, but she didn't *want* to.

"My statement hasn't changed, and neither has my position," Karen said firmly. "I don't have anything to offer."

The detective nodded, but he didn't look entirely convinced. "I expected you would say that. I do want to make you aware, however, that should information on your involvement with any of Mr. DeLucas illegal activities regarding his restaurant become more apparent, you will be seeing me again."

"So be it, but there's nothing to find."

She sounded strong.

She sounded honest.

She felt anything but those things.

Karen had waffled on her warring thoughts for two days since getting confirmation of Dino's arrest. A huge part of her knew what he would want her to do—stay quiet, hidden, and don't draw any sort of attention to the fact she was involved with him in any way.

A smaller part of herself—one that was much louder than the bigger part—didn't care for sensible, smart things.

Perhaps that was why, after dropping her son off at daycare for the day, she had called into work sick, lying that some awful stomach bug had crept up on her overnight. Then, she waffled again. Two hours of going back and forth, of walking down the same Chicago city block, drinking a cold coffee and staring at nothing but the bricks beneath her shoes.

She knew better.

She *did*.

Knowing better didn't stop her from hailing a cab on her third trip of the block, and telling the driver where to take her—the jail.

She only knew which jail was housing Dino because she had made a few calls, looking for the specific detective that had come looking for her. She never left her name or a reason for why she was calling, but she figured if that was the station the man was working out of, that would probably be the same jail Dino was being housed in.

A quick call to the jail at the station confirmed there *was* a prisoner being housed with the name Dino DeLuca.

She figured she could excuse the visit if asked by detectives. She could lie and say she wanted to know why she was being questioned when she hadn't been an employee of Dino's for well over two years. It was a good excuse, she thought.

Karen knew it was stupid.

That still didn't stop her.

She only really realized the gravity of her choice as she stood on the precinct's steps, staring at the large gold lettering above the front entrance. The wide wall-to-wall windows and revolving doors each held the precinct's emblem in the middle, reminding her once again where she was and why she had come there.

While the voice inside told her to turn around and leave while she still could, Karen took a step forward. Then another, and another. She was more focused on making her feet move forward and convincing her inner voice to shut the hell up, rather than staring at what was in front of her.

It was only when a slightly amused, but familiar voice echoed in front of her that Karen finally stopped and looked up.

"Seems it would have been your fault for running into me this time," Theo DeLuca said.

Karen froze on the spot.

To the police, she could have lied.

To Theo?

Probably not so much.

"I—"

Theo's slow smile stopped her from saying something—a lie, probably, as she was getting too good at telling those—but also somehow managed to come off as sympathetic.

"What are you doing here?" Theo asked.

Karen swallowed the sudden lump forming in her throat. "What do you think?"

"I think you're making a stupid mistake."

Ouch.

"You don't know anything, Theo."

He nodded, silently agreeing. "You're right—I don't know very much about my brother at all."

As he said that, he gave her a quick once over, as if to say without actually saying anything at all that he would put her straight into the category of things he didn't know anything about. Karen knew he would be right to do so, too.

"But I do know," Theo continued, "that Dino has made a very careful effort to keep certain things in his life private, and let me say he has done a fucking great job of it."

Her, he meant.

Karen understood his underlying, unspoken words.

"So?" Karen asked.

"So, if you go in there, you're going to ruin all the effort he's made," Theo said quietly. "I think it's probably had a lot to do with the people he doesn't trust, and maybe even a bit about how we grew up. Maybe it's the fact that you're about as much of an outsider as he could get, but away from it all like this, he's managed something much more important where you're concerned."

"And what's that?"

"He's kept you safe."

Oh.

Karen blinked, the sudden stinging sensation in her eyes making her look away to hide the wetness starting to gather there. "I just wanted—"

"Yeah, I get that," Theo interrupted. "It's still not a good idea."

It took a lot—a few more minutes of her standing there trying to internally convince herself otherwise, that what Theo said didn't really matter. But eventually, Karen accepted that what it was, was unfortunately, exactly what it was.

Theo was honest.

Honesty sometimes hurt.

She shouldn't be here.

Dino wouldn't want her here.

"He'll be arraigned on Monday—bail soon after," Theo added after a minute.

Karen wiped at her cheek, nodding. "Okay, thanks."

"Don't come back here, Karen."

She wouldn't.

Even if it killed her.

"Will you let him know—"

Theo laughed, but the sound was colder than she expected. "No, I won't tell him a thing. We're not like that, never have been. Shit, he doesn't even know *I'm* here. Believe it or not, but he wouldn't want me here, either."

Well, then.

That was that.

CHAPTER 22

Dino

"YOUR Honor, my client is—"

The doors to the courtroom swung open, stopping Dino's public defender from arguing his case for bail any further than he had. While he appreciated the lawyer, the guy certainly wasn't like his previous public defender. Mike had been someone Dino was able to trust inexplicably. His new public defender—another man, Carl—didn't have much interest in actually *talking* all that much to his client.

Dino didn't care, as long as the man got him bail.

"Sorry to interrupt," said a tall, well-dressed man.

Dino didn't recognize the man as he pushed beyond the gate, ignoring the glower of the judge from her bench. He thought maybe it was someone for the prosecution's side showing up late, but when the guy made a beeline for Dino's table, he sat a little straighter in his seat. The guy wore a suit that looked like it probably cost him a small fortune, not to mention the glimmering gold cufflinks in the sleeves. Dino only knew an expensive suit when he saw one because he too owned a whole closet full. It was a part of the life, really.

"Can we continue?" the judge asked.

"Two minutes?" the guy asked. "I need just a couple of minutes to explain to my client a few things he wasn't aware of."

The judge didn't look pleased, but muttered, "Make it worth it, Mr. Santiago."

Now that name, Dino *did* recognize.

One of the best defense law firms in the city was Santiago and Sons. He knew of several people who had used the firm because of their ability to get people off on charges, or if not get them off scot-free, then get them one hell of a good deal. They had a reputation for being the best, and they charged like they were the best, too.

Had Dino intended to fight his charges, he probably would have hired the firm. But as it was, he just needed bail, a little time out of jail, and he wasn't ever planning on making it to his next court date, anyway.

Certainly not a fucking trial.

"Dino," the new lawyer said, bending down to speak privately with only him, "nice to meet you, I'm Kon. Your brother hired me. Traffic was a bitch, it won't happen again."

Dino took each of the man's statements in one at a time before he nodded. "Okay."

"And me?" the public defender asked.

Kon shrugged. "Stay or don't, but keep out of my way for the next thirty minutes. He's getting bail or I'm not leaving this courtroom."

Carl sat down in his chair, shutting his briefcase. "Go for it."

"I will," Kon said simply. Then, the man turned back to the judge. "Ready whenever you are, Judge."

The woman behind the bench peered down at Kon with a knowing smile. "You always make it fun, Mr. Santiago."

"You know you can call me Kon, right?"

"And you know I won't," the judge said, laughing. "He's got more money in the bank than even I do. Businesses across the city. Offshore bank accounts. Contacts from here to New York that could move him over the border faster than we could blink. Tell me how he's not a flight risk, please."

Dino blinked, surprised at the judge's blatant knowledge of his contacts. Even the prosecution looked quite pleased, as though the judge had just done their job for them, and he supposed in a way, she had.

"He has a direct hand in one of his businesses," Kon said, "a strip joint in the Heights, not exactly bleeding money or class over there, your Honor. The majority of his businesses have been put in a blind trust since his last arrest. I mean, the ones the Feds haven't shut down on him for one reason or another. Dino hasn't traveled in over four years—not even out of State. He hasn't traveled out of country in *six* years, and his passport was revoked during his last arrest. Three of his accounts are frozen, including the offshore ones. Does he have more—does he have money? Probably, everyone does. He can't live, he can't pay his debts, without money."

"And the contacts?" the judge asked. "The affiliations to criminal organizations across the country?"

"Friends and family don't necessarily mean he's in with the Outfit, too."

"We have every reason to suggest Dino DeLuca *is* a member of the Chicago Mob," the lawyer across the way said, glaring at Kon.

"Give me a recorded video or tape of Dino, admitting his affiliation or of a known made man who says he's a part of any of the organizations in Chicago or even New York. Find me one, show me it, and I'll let you have that, Rudy."

The judge sat a little straighter in her chair, her gaze bouncing between the two lawyers. "All right, play nice, boys. As amusing as it would be to watch you two argue, I have a dinner to get to across town and I'd like to show up in something other than this robe. He's still a flight risk, Kon."

"Twice a day check-ins," Kon said. "Reasonably, you can't refuse Dino bail, even if you put it as high as the sky. He doesn't travel, he doesn't have a lot of means to travel, not without moving funds in a way that would be noticeable, and having a few bad friends doesn't make him a flight risk. Twice a day check-ins to whomever you chose—the prosecution, even."

Dino didn't like that, but he chose not to open his mouth and argue the point.

"I would talk about an ankle monitor," the other lawyer suggested.

Dino did stiffen at that one.

Hell no.

He wasn't wearing one of those things, and they weren't sticking him somewhere he couldn't leave.

Kon must have noticed his change in mood. "No ankle monitor."

It took the judge another few minutes of waffling back and forth, of amusingly eyeing the two lawyers arguing back and forth, before she leaned forward and smacked her hammer down hard enough to silence the room.

"Bail is set at four-hundred-thousand. Check-in once a day with *your* lawyer, Mr. DeLuca, who will then report your check-in to the prosecution. I have no doubt the Feds who are working with the police on this case will have zero problem with confirming your whereabouts from day to day. If you want freedom so much, pay for it."

"Well done," the public defender said to Dino's right.

Kon dismissively glanced over at the guy as he fixed his jacket. "There's a reason profit works better than pro-bono, man. We've got every reason to work sitting in the bank."

"When will the bail be paid?" Dino asked, not caring to involve himself in the other conversation.

"As far as I know, your brother will be on his way to pay for it now. If you're lucky, you'll have those cuffs off before we even leave this building."

Dino frowned. "Theo was here."

"You did hear me say that he hired me, yeah?"

"Yeah, but—"

"Oh, he said he was taking the money from your account, too."

Of course, he did.

Dino sighed, standing when the bailiff came his way. "He should have minded his own business."

Kon eyed Dino curiously. "You're his brother—you *are* his business."

Well, Dino wasn't willing to argue that point, either.

Sure enough, Kon had been right. Before Dino was escorted out of the building and back into the caged van that would deliver him back to the jail, his lawyer showed up with bail papers in hand, handing them over before Dino's cuffs were unlocked.

He rubbed at his wrists. "Thanks."

Kon shrugged. "It's what I do. Next month, we'll be back here to set a trial date."

"Don't bother to drag it on," Dino said.

"I could—it would give us some time. That's always a good thing, Dino."

He didn't need a lot of time.

He just needed a little.

"I'm not going to prison," Dino told the lawyer.

Kon cocked a brow. "Give me time, and you certainly won't, no."

"We don't need time."

He said goodbye to the lawyer, rounded the front steps, and came to an abrupt stop. Standing just a few steps down, apparently waiting for him, were his uncle and his brother. Theo didn't look particularly happy to be there with Ben, but there he was nonetheless.

At the sight of Dino, Ben smiled.

It was one of those chilling smiles Dino had seen many times over the years of his life. A smile that knew exactly what was happening, and displayed how pleased he was for it.

Ben DeLuca was a snake in Dino's grass.

One that had taught him time and time again to trust no one.

He needed to rid himself of that snake.

"Ah, you made bail," Ben said.

Dino stayed expressionless as he walked down the last few steps to meet his uncle and brother. "Seems so."

"Lucky, *nipote*."

Dino didn't think so. "I had a good lawyer."

He passed his brother a look, and Theo gave a nod in response. The brothers' actions were missed by their uncle, thankfully.

"Well," Ben drawled, "it is what it is. You'll have a bit of time— a few months, maybe—before this all comes to a head. How much trouble can you cause in that time? Not very much. Enjoy the bit of freedom you have left, Dino."

Oh, he planned to.

Entirely.

And he took his uncle's words as a challenge accepted.

Dino had watchers—*stalkers*.

It was not easy to lose the officials trailing him damn near constantly, but after a full day of running back and forth across the city, it seemed like he may have done just that. Proverbially patting himself on the back, Dino checked his mirror again, just to be safe.

Nada.

He'd been counting the minutes ticking by since his release days before—watching the seconds count down like a time bomb ready to blow at any moment. The longer he waited, wanting it to be safe, the worse he felt.

Anxiety in his blood.

Loneliness in his heart.

He was without.

Entirely bereft.

Dino had never really understood how totally *alone* he felt before. He'd done quite well on his own without the infliction of bringing others into his world. He'd done perfectly fine being his own person, living in his own private hell.

Even if it was a hell, it was his.

He owned it.

And there he was, so fucking alone.

Not for much longer.

It was stupid; it would have been better had he waited a while longer before going to see Karen and his son, just to be safe. Yet, the ache in his soul was never really gone. His usual methods for distracting himself weren't working. Not work, jogging, or filling his mind with useless things to keep his attention on anything but the things he wanted the most.

None of it worked.

That was why, the very second he had the chance, the very moment he knew it was safe, he had found himself racing across town. A single look at his clock told him exactly where Karen would be—leaving work in five minutes. She had an hour before she'd have to pick up Junior from the daycare, and then like every night, she would go home with their son and cook supper.

She, like him, was a creature of habit.

Even when her world was falling apart, she kept her routine.

Dino put his car in park in the lot of the studio where Karen worked damn near at the same time as she came out the back doors. Her gaze landed on his car almost immediately, and her walk stumbled for a split second. The windows on his Bentley were too dark to see inside, but she had to know it was him.

How many people did she know that drove a white Bentley

with black windows?

Just him.

Karen didn't even hesitate, she crossed the lot quickly, her dress fluttering around her legs as she jogged his way. He thought she would go to the passenger side door, but she came to his, throwing it open and climbing inside without a single word.

She landed in his lap, and Dino closed the door.

In that moment, the rest of the world ceased to exist.

With her in his arms, her scent all around him, and the windows of his car too dark for the outside world to see in, they were all that mattered.

They were all that existed.

Karen buried her face in Dino's neck, and he held her a little tighter. He didn't think the position could be all that comfortable for her, especially not with the steering wheel driving into her back, but she didn't make a single complaint.

"Give it to me," he murmured.

She sucked in a hard breath, and he braced himself for the impact of whatever might come next. Her anger, probably. Her bitterness. Anything.

Karen had every right to it all.

"Come on," he said when she stayed silent.

Finally, Karen shook her head. "You said I wouldn't have to do this alone, Dino."

He had.

And she wouldn't.

"Look at me." Dino grabbed Karen's face, tilting her head up so he could stare her in the eyes. The tears were there, fresh and ready to fall, but she didn't let them. His thumbs stroked her cheeks as he kissed her mouth once, then twice. "We're going to be just fine."

"How many years?"

He hesitated, but answered. "Over twenty."

"*Twenty.*"

"Over, Karen."

The sound that broke free from her chest was *raw*—pain-filled, aching, and low. It cut him straight through the bone and into his heart, but he welcomed that pain. He deserved it.

"That's not going to happen," he promised.

"Don't say things that you want, say what is *true*."

Dino nodded, and kissed her again. "I'm not going to prison."
That was going to be his mantra for the next little while.
And no matter what, he was going to make it happen.

CHAPTER 23

Dino

THERE was a side to Karen that no one really got to see, and if they did see it, they couldn't possibly understand it enough to appreciate it. It had been her bright soul, shining straight through the darkness of Dino's that had drawn him in—her perpetual happiness, always seeing the good, and never indulging the bad.

Yes, that had drawn him in, but her strength was the part of her that amazed him the most.

He made a great effort never to show his weaknesses, to never appear less than those around him. And yet, in the face of adversary, in the midst of her pain, Karen never blinked a lash. No one would ever know how hard she struggled, or how much her heart hurt, because she just kept going.

Even knowing how her world must have felt like a hurricane because of him and his actions, Dino watched her from the sidelines as she picked their son up from daycare, chatted to the workers like nothing was amiss, and went about her routine with Junior at her side. She played silly games with their son, kept him distracted, and cooked supper while Dino had Junior in his lap. She went about her day without mention of any problem or pain.

She didn't let her son see their chaos.

She didn't let the world know her concerns.

That *amazed* him.

Her strength amazed him.

Dino knew, one day, he was going to sit his son down and

explain how incredible the boy's mother really was. Mothers were so often overlooked—they were the people who wiped faces and tucked babies into beds at night. They were constant figures of love and warmth.

Karen was so much more than just that for Dino and Junior.

He wanted his son to know someday.

He resolved himself with the knowledge that he would be there to tell him.

No matter what it took to do so.

At the same time, for all Karen's strength and perseverance, Dino was all too aware that underneath the brave face she put on, there was just a woman who needed to breathe, who wanted to feel safe, loved, and needed. He'd seen those parts of her, too, and that was exactly why he knew they existed.

So he grabbed her a bottle of wine from the fridge, a red, deep liquor with just enough sweetness to let her drink it fast if she wanted. He drew her a bath, hot enough to steam the mirrors and with enough bubbles that they were spilling over the edge.

She didn't question his motives when he pulled her into the bathroom after she'd put their son down to bed. She let him pull her dress off, took the bottle of wine when he offered it, and then she pulled him into the hot bath with her when she was ready.

That was where he found himself, surrounded by the strength of one terribly amazing woman, and he soaked that in for all it was worth.

He didn't deserve her.

He was still going to keep her.

"I love you," Dino whispered the words in her ear.

Karen's profile showcased her soft, knowing smile. "You don't say it a lot."

"I show it; you said that to me once."

"You do."

"I'll say it more often," he promised.

Every day.

Whenever she wanted.

He didn't mind.

Dino took the dangling wine bottle from Karen's hand and sat it to the bathroom floor when she asked him to, knowing she would never drink enough that she might not wake up if Junior needed her in the night. She was smart in that way—a good mother, really.

She was still a little tipsy, though, just enough to feel it.

That was good, too.

He kissed the side of her neck when she rested back against his chest, and for a short while, the rest of the world and all the problems in it went away again. He'd been making a special effort to ignore his growing erection—a problem he could never quite solve when Karen was naked and close to him—but he was becoming painfully more aware of it each and every time she shifted in his lap.

Then, without a word, her hand was slipping under the water and between her thighs. She lifted, making the water slosh around the edge of the tub and more bubbles fall down to the floor. The tub was really too small for them to be playing in it together like they were, but he wasn't about to complain.

Dino felt Karen's fingers wrap around the base of his cock, and she fitted him right where he needed to be. She lowered back down on his member with a slowness that damn near killed him in the best way. She was so hot from the water, her sex slick and clenching around him as she took him all the way in, until she was seated back in his lap, a perfect fit.

She stayed still like that for a while, a gentle shudder crawling over her skin every so often when his muscles flexed and his cock jerked inside her body.

"That's better," Karen murmured.

Dino chuckled, his hands finding the damp strands of her hair to pile high on the top of her head. "Yeah?"

"Been too long."

On that, he agreed.

It was always too long.

He tugged her head to the side, keeping his hand firmly tangled in her hair, as he kissed a path over the side of her neck. The wetness on her skin tasted heavenly, and he paused over her pulse point, feeling the rapid thrum of her heartbeat against his tongue.

There, he felt her life.

That radiating, beautiful, amazing life.

"Can we just stay like this for a while?" she asked softly.

How would he refuse her that?

"For as long as you want," he said.

"Is forever too long?"

Dino laughed. "Someone down the hall might not like that when he wakes up wanting food in the morning."

Karen turned to look at him, pouting. "Damn."

He kissed her frown away. "I can make it good for now, though."

That pout turned into a sexy little smile. "Let's do that, then."

Always.

His hand stayed in her hair, while his other dipped below the bubbly water between her thighs. He found the softness of her sex with his fingertips, gliding his digits over the folds and the base of his cock where he had her filled. He liked feeling that—he liked seeing it even better—but feeling it was pretty fucking good, too.

Then he traced her clit, measured and slow, small circles that he knew would get her shaking in no time at all. That way, he could hear all her sweet cries and taste more salt on her skin when she came.

Karen sucked in a soft breath, never lifting from his lap but instead, rotating her hips right where she sat, moving in time with his fingers against her clit while her fingernails dug into the muscles of his thighs.

He didn't think that would do much for him, but it really did. Each tremor of her body, every clench of her muscles, made his spine tingle and his breaths quicken. He kept that tempo up, letting her rotate her pussy into his cock while he played with her clit until she was a shaking, breathless mess in his lap.

"Oh, my God," Karen mumbled as she came.

So sweet.

So high and pretty.

Dino kissed a path along the delicate line of her jaw as she came back down from that first ride. "I don't think God had much to do with this here, sweetheart."

Karen laughed, sounding spun and blissed. "You don't believe in that sort of thing anyway, do you?"

No, he worshipped someone else entirely.

From the moment Dino had gotten the cuffs taken off him and his proverbial freedom had been given back, a sense of calm and waiting had settled over him.

It was back to business as usual with the Outfit.

His trial date was set a month after his release—the trial was still a few months away, yet.

It didn't affect him, not like people might think that it should.

He had far too many other things to worry about.

Going back to prison was not one of them.

He'd been so calm, so collected, that when he felt those first wisps of panic well deep in his heart, he had been surprised to feel them at all. He'd been doing so well not entertaining the thought, not bothering with it in any way. It was easier to do that, rather than sit and stew.

Those first wisps of panic came as he sat at the Outfit boss's table, eating a meal with people he didn't give less than a shit about. He'd barely partook in the conversation, barely bothered with the people, his boss, or even his family at all.

He realized in those moments, when no one engaged him, either, that whether he was there, in another country somewhere away from the judicial system of America, stuck behind bars, or dead in the ground …

Nothing would change.

These people would still be the same.

The same hateful, greedy, excessive, awful people that they were. They would still hide secrets for one another, still turn a blind eye to the boy with bruises down his back, and pretend like the little girl didn't cry for her mother after they'd murdered her.

Nothing about him being there or not being there would change.

Dino watched his brother engage with Damian Rossi and the hitman's cousin, Tommas. He noticed Ben listening in to the conversation, and looking displeased that the friendship between those families was still there.

He considered his brother, and how difficult it would be for Theo to maintain his position and be safe at the same time, if Dino was not there to assert *his* position and rank on the people around him. Without a doubt, Theo would be left contending with people like Ben and their uncle's underlings—the Artino family, for example—for control.

And if Theo wasn't able to assert his position and control, then he would lose it.

At the least.

The more likely scenario was that his brother might find himself in a casket because he was disposable—a way to the top.

Perhaps Dino had been so … caught up in his own world and problems that he'd forgotten the people he'd protected for so many years. His decision had been cemented long ago on the prison thing—he wasn't going back there. He didn't care if he had to run, or what it was that he needed to do, but he promised his son to be there for his second birthday, and he was damn well going to be.

But what difference would leaving do?

His loss would be nothing to these people.

It would do nothing for his brother.

And even his estranged sister, Lily, would be left to the wolves with Dino not there to keep *her* freedom safe from those who might use it to gain something for themselves.

He sat there a while longer, listening to the conversations and hating them all the more because nothing would change for them—they were all puzzle pieces, some pawns, others kings and queens.

He wondered …

What would happen if he started making a few moves of his own?

Dino waved for his brother to come inside his home office before his attention went back to the person on the other end of the call.

"But, Dino—"

"It's time to come home, Lily," he told his sister.

She was young, difficult, combative, and stubborn.

She was pretty, smart, different, and soulfully free.

Those were all things he knew held his sister back, but also might let her fly someday. He was going to make sure she had every chance to do that, even if he had to clip her wings to make it happen.

He didn't expect his sister to understand.

He wasn't going to explain his motives.

She only had to *listen.*

"Two months," he said firmly, "and if you're not home in Chicago by the end of that time, little one, I will come looking for you. Do you understand that?"

Lily huffed on the other end of the call. "I get it."

"You don't like it, though."

"I've done everything you wanted. I followed the rules. I don't under—"

"It's time for you to come home," he repeated simply.

Another frustrated sigh answered him back before the phone call ended. Dino didn't bother to call his sister back, she probably wouldn't pick up anyway. She was troubled in that way, and she'd been using her trip to backpack across Europe as a way to run from her past and the problems she didn't want to face.

Problems like the Outfit and their murdered parents.

He hated bringing her back down to reality, but he didn't have a choice.

He had things to do—people to care for when he wouldn't be able to.

Lily was one of those people.

Another one of those people was sitting in the chair on the other side of his desk.

Theo cocked a brow when Dino slammed the phone down. "You're calling Lily back home?"

"My right to do so."

"Never said it wasn't. Why now?"

Dino shrugged. "Seems like the right time."

"Does Ben know?"

"No. He'll go looking for a man to marry her to the moment her feet hit Chicago soil. That isn't going to happen—not the way he wants it to, anyway."

Theo's gaze narrowed. "What's that supposed to mean?"

Dino didn't bother to explain it.

He wasn't required to explain himself.

He never had, anyway.

"What are you doing here?" Dino asked.

Theo rested back into the chair, his aloof disposition becoming all the more apparent as he watched Dino in that silent way of his. The two brothers were far too alike for their own good, although neither of them would admit it.

"Stopped by to make sure everything was good while you were waiting on bail," Theo said.

Dino nodded. "Thanks."

"Mailed some of the stuff you had sitting on your desk."

"Great."

"Ran into Karen outside of the jail and stopped her from making the mistake of going inside and getting her name put on a record of visitation for you."

Dino froze in his chair, his gaze sliding from the clock on the wall to his brother's stone-cold features. "Theo—"

"Do you not trust me, Dino? Is that why you've never told me about them?"

His throat felt so fucking tight.

A part of him wanted to distract Theo—to piss him off and get him out of his face, even if it burned more bridges between them, but stopped him from asking questions that Dino had no intention of ever answering.

Still, he answered.

"It's not about trust," Dino admitted.

"Then what is it?"

"They're not a part of this—they've never been a part of this. They're mine, and I won't ever put them at risk like everything else in my life is, Theo. It's not about whether or not I trust you. It's everyone else around us, it's the people who've hurt me and you and Lily over and over again, just because they could. Don't ask me if it's because I don't trust you, when you know the monsters that live inside my head. You live with the same monsters I do, we just deal with them in different ways, Theo."

Theo stayed silent for a long while, then he leaned forward in the chair and nodded at the phone. "So when is Lily coming home?"

And just like that, the conversation was over.

It was the DeLuca way.

CHAPTER 24

Karen

"HE'S too little to go on any of these rides," Karen said, looking around the carnival at the Pier.

"Not all," Dino replied, shifting his son on his hip. "And some he can go on with us."

"Sure, but—"

"It's a fun night for him. He'll be so tired by the time we get him home. He'll sleep all night and you won't hear a thing. Maybe you'll even get to sleep in tomorrow."

Well, Karen did like the sound of that.

J was an odd child sometimes. He would wake up at the very crack of dawn, ready and revving to go. Sometimes it didn't seem like it mattered *when* he went to bed, either. Seven at night, or much later, he still woke up far too early for it to be normal.

Karen's normal, anyway.

"Not sure that'll make much of a difference, Dino," Karen admitted.

"We'll see. Let's find something to do. You hungry?"

She nodded, as it was well past supper and Dino's visit had been a surprise. Not that surprise visits were anything particularly new for him—he did it all the time. That night, however, she had just got home and was about to start cooking something when he walked in the door talking about a date night.

Date night?

Karen and Dino had *never* been on a proper date, and she didn't think their occasional late nights with popcorn, wine, and movies on the couch really constituted what was a proper date. She liked those nights with him, sure, she loved them even, but they weren't actually *dates*.

And being out and about in a very bustling, public place with Dino felt almost ... strange.

"Is everything okay?" Karen asked as they approached a food truck.

The lights of the pier and the carnival lit up the sky, making their son distracted at every little turn. Little J kept trying to climb higher on his father's shoulders to see more. Dino eventually just shifted the boy around so he was sitting on his father's shoulders before he turned to answer Karen.

"Everything is fine, sweetheart." Dino stepped up to order. "What do you want?"

Karen looked over the menu and settled for something that would fill her up, but not make her stomach too heavy. If they were going to take the baby on rides—even child rides—she needed to be careful.

She had never done well with motion sickness.

After she'd given Dino her order, he placed his own, something for the baby, and then paid. They stepped off to the side to wait for their order to be filled.

"Are you sure?" Karen asked. "Nothing's changed?"

Dino passed Karen a look before he reached out and snagged her by the wrist, drawing her closer into his side. "You're worrying about nothing. Enjoy the night out. You don't get to do that much, Karen."

Fine.

That was true enough.

It still didn't settle her concerns.

Again, as much as she liked being close to Dino, as much as she enjoyed being *normal* with Dino and acting like the couple they were, it was all a little strange. They didn't go out in public together. They weren't seen even in the same vicinity together.

And for good reason.

Sure, he had been extra careful that night, it seemed, making sure no one was following him, showing up in a rental car, and taking the long way to the Pier, which actually just meant he drove aimlessly to make sure no one was following him.

He'd still been careful.

But she had to wonder ...

"What if someone sees us?" Karen asked quietly.

Dino kissed the top of her head. "Not worried about it."

His flippant reply was clearly meant to placate her, but she wasn't sure he was telling her the truth.

"I wanted to do something with you two tonight," Dino said quietly, drawing Karen's attention back to him. "Can't I do that?"

"You've never done it before."

Dino smiled. "Not for lack of wanting to, Karen."

Oh.

"Besides," he added, "a lot of people I know are distracted by a very important man's birthday party tonight, and I needed a break. Something other than holing myself up in an apartment with you and Junior. This is good, right?"

"It's great," Karen said.

She still worried.

She wanted normal.

Of course, she did.

But she didn't want to be scared of it, either.

Soon, the food was ready, their son's attention was snagged by a waiting hotdog, and Karen decided to let her worries go as much as she could.

Dino wanted them to have a good night, to have some fun together.

She wasn't going to spoil that with nonsense.

"Oh, my God," Karen mumbled when Dino sat the tiny boxes of take-out in front of her on the coffee table. "Chinese, too—you're a life saver."

He dropped a quick kiss to the very top of her head, lingering there for a while as she opened the first container to find chow mein noodles inside.

Her very favorite.

"You said you were having a bad day," he murmured.

Karen shrugged. "Busy day."

He dropped to the couch beside her, grabbing his own container and opening it up. Chopsticks in hand, Dino dug in while Karen ate happily beside him.

"Tell me about it," Dino said.

Karen sighed. "Client after client at the studio."

"You like it there, don't you?"

"Love it. I was lucky to get the job. Some days are just harder than others. You don't get to pick and choose your clients most of the time, unless someone specifically asks for you. The boss kind of shoved a harder-to-deal-with mother on me, and yeah."

Dino grunted under his breath. "Shitty."

"I did okay."

"That all?"

"No, Junior bit someone at daycare. They told me if he keeps that up, he'll lose his spot."

Dino's brow lifted as he looked over to Karen, a million and one questions in his eyes. "Really?"

"Which part do you find hard to believe—the biting, or the kicking him out?"

"The kicking him out bit."

Yeah, Karen found that hard to believe, too.

Their son didn't bite people every chance he got, unless he was put under stressful situations or someone tried to hold him still, and he really did prefer to play alone, rather than with other children. She had a sneaking suspicion that the daycare was attempting to get Junior in situations where he needed to play more with other children. She understood why. It was good for his developmental skills, and team building, she supposed.

Still, the toddler likely wasn't having it.

"I just apologized," Karen said lamely.

"For what? You can't control where his teeth go."

"Apparently, I am supposed to."

Dino scoffed. "That's fucking stupid."

"I thought so."

"Listen, if they kick him out, we'll figure something else out," Dino said.

Karen's chopstick froze on the way to her mouth, and she

looked over at Dino. "Oh, will you be calling around to local daycares for me to get him a spot last minute?"

Dino sat his container of food down. "Karen."

"Well?"

"Come on."

She scowled at her food, knowing none of this was really Dino's fault, but her stress was manifesting outwardly and he was the closest person for her to take her anger out on. He didn't deserve it, as far as that went, but she didn't know how else to deal.

"Sorry," Karen said quietly.

In a flash, Dino had taken her food from her, sat it aside, and then he pulled her into his lap without a word. There, the stress seemed to wash away, and she was okay.

"I try to help all the time," Dino said, resting his chin on the top of her head.

He wasn't lying.

He did help, when Karen would let him.

She rarely took money from him, and he offered that a lot. He often came over at the drop of a hat when she asked him to, just because she needed a break. And then there were lots of nights like this one where she hadn't eaten, she'd been stressed out to the max, and he'd showed up just because he heard the exhaustion in her voice over a phone call.

"You do help," Karen said. "I shouldn't have said that."

"I'd like to help *more*," Dino admitted.

"Giving me money—"

"Not you, the baby."

Karen rolled her eyes. "It's the same thing, because you mean for me to control the cash."

Dino shrugged. "*For* the baby."

"You're not being sneaky enough about this. I can see right through it."

"Fine," Dino said heavily. "But it's right there. All you have to do is ask."

Not yet.

"He understands he is not allowed to bite people," she said to herself.

"Maybe he's picking up on your stress lately, too."

That was a good point.

Then, Dino added just as quickly, "Why don't you ... I don't know, take some time off, get away with him for a bit?"

He'd offered the suggestion rather carefully, but it felt laced with something Karen couldn't quite put her finger on.

"What do you mean?" Karen asked.

Dino made a dismissive sound, almost as if to make it seem like it wasn't a big deal when he said, "You know, use some of your vacation time for whatever. Say it's an emergency, they won't know the difference. Hell, the cabin is an hour and a half away, out in the middle of nowhere, and private. You could stay there for a while even. Get away from the world."

That sounded wonderful, actually.

It was probably exactly what she and the baby needed.

Still, something in Dino's voice was just … *off*.

She sat up in his lap, and pushed off him to then sit back on her own side of the couch. Dino watched her from the side, and by the look on his face, Karen knew she had been right.

"What's going on?" she asked.

A month ago, they had gone to the carnival, and had a great night out with their son. Sure, summer was here, and the cabin would be a great way to spend it with her son, but she didn't think that was what Dino was trying to get her to do.

Something just told her to look deeper.

Something inside demanded she ask more questions.

Dino met her gaze, never dropping it as he said, "Everything is fine."

"Here, sure, but tell me about there."

There was the Outfit.

There was his other life.

There was people he rarely talked about.

There was a strange and unknown place to her.

A tic worked in Dino's jaw, an action Karen recognized as his anxiety. He had very few tells, but that was absolutely one of them.

"Dino," Karen pressed.

"If I wanted to send you away for a while, just to be safe, would you do it for me, no questions asked?"

She would.

"I'd want a reason," Karen said.

Dino nodded once. "I'm not going back to prison."

"You keep saying that—the media coverage on your case thinks differently."

He didn't look like he particularly cared.

"I'm not going back there," he said firmly. "But I also can't just leave, either. Things need to be right—good—for the people I might have to leave behind."

Karen blinked. "Leave?"

"Not you," he murmured.

"Leave," she repeated, not posing it as a question that time.

"Not J, either."

"Leave where?"

Dino didn't answer that one. "Would you go for me if I asked you to?"

"How long?"

"A couple months."

"I only have a couple of weeks of vacation to use. I'll lose my job."

Dino reached for his blazer he'd left hanging over the back of the couch, and pulled out a manila envelope from the inner pocket. The last time she had seen a package like that, it had been bursting with money.

"Dino …"

"Junior always comes first, right?" Dino asked. "You don't need to work, and you don't have to like it, but you do need to use this and whatever else I give. It's for him, it's not for you."

Fuck.

He had her there.

And he knew it.

"What's going to happen, Dino, that you need to send us away?" Karen dared to ask.

"I'm not entirely sure yet."

For some reason, maybe it was because of the tenor his voice took on, she believed him.

CHAPTER 25

Dino

IT was such a warm May day that Dino wanted to enjoy it outside, but the chilly attitude of his company was making the nice weather less than pleasant.

"If you're going to sit there and glare at me all goddamn day, go find something else to do, little one," Dino muttered.

Lily, his younger sister, continued to glower at him from her position on the porch bench. Dino tried to act like her mood wasn't bothering him all that much by resting further into his reclining lawn chair and staring up at the near cloudless sky.

His sister was due her anger.

He wouldn't deny that.

After all, it had been him who demanded two months ago, that she come home from traveling Europe without so much as an explanation. And with a threat to track her down himself if needed to boot. She hadn't appreciated that very much.

Dino did what he had to.

Well, what he was *going* to be doing.

Soon.

It was all to her best interests, but he knew explaining it all to Lily would be a waste of his time. She was too stubborn—too bitter towards him, and the entire Outfit as a whole—to really listen to what he would try and tell her.

So he wasn't going to try at all.

"You want to grab some grub?" Dino asked. "Take-out for

supper, maybe?"

Lily stayed silent.

So was her way, it seemed.

Since she had arrived home the week before, all she ever did was glare at him, refuse to speak, and *if* she did talk to him, it was almost always to call him a bastard.

"Should save that energy and anger up," Dino said under his breath.

Apparently, Lily had heard him. "Why?"

"You're going to need it soon, little one."

More than she knew …

Damian Rossi was an interesting man—a *dangerous* man, to be sure, but interesting nonetheless. His history with Dino had been long, and quite far-reaching, if he were honest.

It started when they were just kids.

Well, Damian had been a kid.

Dino had been an older teenager at the time.

Damian struck up a friendship with Theo all those years ago that had seemed to weather the storms of life that was the Outfit and mafia. As the boys had grown into men, Damian had moved more towards the Rossi side of the Outfit, while Theo stayed firmly stuck in the DeLuca side. Still, they remained friends.

As kids, they'd chummed around a lot. Theo, Damian, and Lily—because she was never far behind her older brother after their parents' murder, which meant she was often shoved in the friends' messes, too.

Neither boy seemed to mind.

Now, as an Outfit man, Damian was … well, as Dino had said before, dangerous.

Working as a personal hitman for the boss, and doing work on his cousin, Tommas', crew, Damian had certainly earned his spot. But if Dino knew *anything* about the man that he had learned over the years, it was that one thing never changed about Damian's personality.

The man liked the shadows.

He liked being unknown—*unseen*.

They called him Ghost for a reason, and it was a good one.

Over the years, Dino had taken inventory of the people around him, of the many facets of life inside each of the four Outfit families. There were certainly personality traits of each person that might be considered a weakness, or even a strength, depending on how a person looked at it.

Dino only looked at what he could use.

Ben had taught him that in his many lessons.

Damian was someone Dino could use for more than one reason.

"You're going to marry my sister," Dino said.

Across his desk, Damian's head snapped up from the file of information he was overlooking that had as many details about Lily DeLuca and her life as Dino could put together on his sister. She was going to hate him for this; she would fight him tooth and fucking nail on it, but what was done, would be done.

Men in the Outfit got to make those plays and calls for the women.

Nobody said it was fair.

Nobody said it was nice.

Nobody had to fucking like it.

But God knew if Dino didn't do this for his sister—give her somebody he knew had history with her, someone she wouldn't be able to hate once she got to know him, and somebody who was capable of caring for her and keeping her safe—Jesus, who would be left to do it?

Ben, probably.

Their uncle was already looking for someone to marry her off to since she arrived back in Chicago. That was just how Ben made his moves in the Outfit, by manipulating those he could, and using the backs of others to get where he needed to be.

Isn't that what you're about to do, too?

Dino ignored his inner voice.

His was for the betterment of many people, not only himself.

Ben never thought of others when he made moves in a game he never really understood how to play fairly.

"What?" Damian asked.

"You owe me."

A life for a life—that was how the mafia worked.

Damian had owed his life to Dino for a long time, ever since a younger Damian had gotten himself into some trouble that Dino stepped in on to save the guy's ass. He took the rap for Damian killing a made man, got the guy out of it, and he went on to do half decent things with his mafia career.

"It's time to pay up," Dino added.

And by that, he meant Damian would pay up by marrying Lily.

By keeping her safe.

By making her happy.

By doing whatever he needed to do so that she had whatever she needed.

"It seems pretty simple, doesn't it?" Dino said. "And you know, with all the attention from the boss on you lately, you should be careful."

Dino wasn't the type to manipulate others—he didn't like to play on the fears of men around him because his whole life had been nothing but that, and it wasn't fair to play that game with people when they didn't know they too were playing it.

He didn't have a choice here.

"Seems the boss has really taken a liking to you," Dino said, leaning forward. "Some people don't like that—Ben, Riley, the usual. You know what happens in the Outfit when a man is going somewhere that another man doesn't want him to go, don't you?"

Damian didn't blink, his features cold and schooled. "I know—stop the man by whatever means necessary."

"Seems you have a lot to think about."

Yeah, over the years, he'd watched people like Damian Rossi.

He learned things about them. Things he could use if he ever needed to.

That time had finally come.

Damian didn't like attention, and he liked being free to do his own thing, even if that freedom came at a cost where others lost for him to win. He didn't like others making moves on his life that would put him in a position where he didn't want to be, and he didn't mind culling people who spoke out against him.

A few choice words, a bit of manipulation on Dino's part, and he could already see that Damian wasn't about to let the men around him make choices on his future within the Outfit without his say so.

"I don't care what you do about it, really," Dino said, "as long as your end of the bargain with me regarding Lily and the marriage is kept."

Damian didn't reply.

Dino didn't really need him to.

What was done, was already done.

Just like that.

So easy.

"Except, of course, Ben," Dino added after a moment. "You see, in order to keep Lily safe, Ben needs to go. He'll be vocal about his dislike of you, and of this whole thing, really. And as it is, he already doesn't like you very much because the boss is fond of you. Either I can worry about that, or you can, Damian."

"And what about the people who will look to retaliate for Ben?" Damian asked.

Dino shrugged. "Deal with it, I suppose."

"You make it sound easy."

Wasn't it?

Damian was a decent guy underneath his dangerous exterior, but he was just like everybody else in the Outfit. For the betterment of themselves, for their family.

The only difference was Dino had effectively just made Lily and Theo a part of Damian's family, too.

He'd have to push the younger hitman along, force his hand, probably, to do what needed to be done, but Damian would do it.

He was good like that.

And as long as Lily and Theo had a place to land softly when all of it was said and done, then Dino figured the blood that would stain his hands—and even Damian's—would be worth it in the end.

Dino wasn't going back to prison.

He was still sticking to that, no matter what.

No way in hell would he leave his family out to dry at the end, either.

This was just the beginning.

"Dino."

The call of his name drew Dino's attention up from the glass of wine he was holding. Terrance stared at him expectantly from the other end of the table, waiting as the boss usually did for his man to speak up when he knew there was news to share.

After all, Dino couldn't make all the important calls regarding his family without vetting some of them through the boss.

The marriage had been just one.

Terrance had thought it would be good to ... announce it.

Show it off.

Make it known.

Dino wasn't that kind of man, but he did what the boss wanted. That was just how the Outfit worked.

"Yeah, boss?" Dino asked.

"I think now is a good time to share the news you have."

All eyes in the room turned on him.

Familiar faces.

Waiting people.

Only three or so really mattered to him in some way. Their reactions would be important, and even dangerous.

Ben was one.

Theo was another.

Damian was there as well, though he already knew what was coming.

Dino lifted his glass, smiling, though it felt odd to do it. "In a couple months, there will be some big changes for the DeLuca family."

Ben's expression hardened as he looked down the table at Dino. "How so, *nipote?*"

There it was ...

"This is good," Terrance said, "you'll enjoy this, Ben."

Dino doubted it, but he kept talking because he had to. "A marriage, between Lily and Damian, near the end of summer. It's settled—right, boss?"

He only needed Terrance's permission, after all.

Ben wouldn't matter, then.

He couldn't say a thing.

It still worried Dino.

"A marriage?" Ben asked quietly. "Between—"

"It's fantastic," Terrance cut in. "They're a good match."

Damian said nothing from where he sat, staring blankly at the wall like he wasn't even in the room.

"Yes," Ben echoed, though his gaze cut to Dino, promising a conversation later that probably wouldn't be pleasant. "A good match, sure."

Thirty minutes later, Dino left the table, ready to leave the dinner. His uncle met him at the door, and he wasn't even surprised.

"What the fuck are you doing?" Ben hissed.

Dino had known full and well his uncle would be pissed.

He expected this.

"It's settled," he said, echoing his earlier words. "You heard the boss, Ben."

"I'm the head of DeLuca family," Ben practically snarled. "I make those kinds of calls. You know I've been looking for someone—"

"You don't care about Lily, or what she wants. You would marry her off to the first asshole that offered you the best price, regardless of what he was like behind closed doors. If you think I'd let you do that to my sister, think again, Ben. It's *settled*. You don't get a say."

Ben glared, his hand twitching at his side.

Had Dino been a younger man, had they been in a different place, he had no doubt his uncle would have struck him down to the ground right then.

Old habits were hard to change.

He knew he had poked a bear—he'd woken up a monster in his uncle.

It'd been a while since he really feared that monster.

He figured this time, by the time Ben reacted, it would already be too late.

Things were already in motion.

Dino had rolled the ball.

He just needed to keep it moving and the course would run out for Ben.

Eventually.

"You'll regret making a fool of me like this," Ben said coldly.

"I doubt it," Dino replied.

His uncle stalked off, leaving him alone in the hallway. Well, it seemed he wasn't entirely alone. At the other side, he could see his brother standing in the shadows.

Theo had watched the whole scene unfold.

Good.

Dino figured it was time his brother started filling in all those blanks they had left between one another throughout the years.

CHAPTER 26

Karen

"HERE, let me help with those," Dino said as he dropped his overnight bag in the corner of the kitchen.

Karen didn't have time to refuse his offer, she really didn't need help peeling the potatoes or cutting up the rest of the vegetables, but he was already behind her, his large hands slipping the items from her grasp and getting to work.

Dino's lips skimmed the back of Karen's neck before he kissed her right over the same spot. She smiled. Slowly but surely, he went to work peeling the potatoes and dropping them in the colander to be washed.

He barricaded her against the sink from behind, she realized.

Karen liked his closeness, and the surprise visit, so she didn't say a thing, instead resting her head back on his large shoulder while he concentrated on his work.

"What are we cooking?" Dino asked.

"Stew."

"A little hot for stew."

"I need to go grocery shopping," Karen explained. "I had the ingredients to make this."

Dino chuckled. "Ah."

"Since when do you visit on a Monday night?"

For the last few weeks that she had been staying at the cabin, Dino had come to visit on a fairly regular basis. Almost always on the weekend, and usually closer to the evening. He didn't stay much longer than a day, maybe a day and a half, but it was enough to keep their son happy, and Karen was enjoying her time away from the city and life.

Truthfully, she was considering not going back at all.

But that was another thing to deal with at another time.

"Since I decided to get away from the woman in my house driving me crazy," Dino muttered.

Karen turned into a block of ice in his arms. "I beg your pardon?"

There was a *woman* in his *house?*

Jealousy flared to life like a raging inferno determined to devastate Karen's insides. She never questioned Dino on his fidelity to her, if only because he seemed to have so little interest in others—especially women—and he'd never given her any indication that he was seeing other people.

Why would he give her that indication?

He made damn sure to mention she wasn't to see anyone else but him.

She expected the same.

"Wow, I can *feel* you wanting to kill me right now," Dino said, chuckling.

Karen spun slowly in his arms to face him, and Dino let her, dropping the knife and potato in his hands. She came to a stop, never breaking eye contact once she held his gaze. He reached behind her, turned the tab on, and washed his hands and all the while, she continued to glare at him, silently wishing for him to feel all the anger about to spew from her mouth.

"I beg your pardon?" she repeated.

It came out a heck of a lot calmer the second time around.

Dino didn't look the least bit fazed. If anything, he looked *amused*. Karen was two seconds away from smacking that infuriating smirk off of his face.

"My sister—*Lily*—is at my place until her wedding," Dino said, his grin growing as Karen's stiff shoulders began to deflate. "We don't get along. Think how I've mentioned my brother and me to be, but ten times worse. She's young, stubborn, and spoiled. I did that last one by letting her do whatever the hell she wanted for years, so I have no one to blame but myself."

Karen took a deep breath. "Your sister."

"She's not happy, but she wasn't ever going to be anyway.

Although, I have to say, she is happier."

Wait, what?

"She's getting married but she's not happy?" Karen asked, her brow furrowing. "Why would she get married if—"

"The wedding is coming right up—I'm hoping she gets her shit sorted and whatever issues she's got with her fiancé put to bed before it gets here."

Karen just stared at him. "She's got issues with her fiancé?"

That didn't sound like a very good relationship.

Dino shrugged. "All women who are told to marry a man they don't know very well aren't going to be very pleasant to deal with for a while. At least, that's what someone told me."

"*What?*"

Her remark came out so damned sharp that even Dino froze and glanced down at her.

"Shit, forgot to mention that, huh?"

Karen didn't quite know how to respond. "You're *making* your sister marry someone?"

"To be fair, they've got history. It's just *old*—like when they were kids, old—history."

"Is that … normal?"

She'd posed the question so vaguely that she wasn't sure if Dino would even know what she was asking, but thankfully, he seemed to pick up on her intent.

"In the Outfit, it's more common than you would care to know," Dino admitted.

"That's awful. No wonder she's unhappy, Dino!"

He *shrugged* again.

"Dino!" Karen exclaimed at his lack of concern or care.

"If *I* don't do this for my sister, then someone else will, and they won't think about her at all," Dino explained quietly.

"But—"

"I picked someone she can't hate, and someone who has history with her that's sure to influence his side of things. It might take a little while, but it'll all work itself out, I'm sure."

Karen felt like she had entered an alternate universe. "I don't like this."

"You don't have to, really."

Well, then …

"Where's the baby?" he asked when Karen stayed quiet.

"Having his afternoon nap."

Dino smiled. "Good, good."

Then, his strong, warm hands started traveling up her bare thighs under the skirt of the flimsy summer dress she was wearing. His brown gaze held hers as his hands moved between her thighs, finding the sweet spot between her legs and stroking her through her thong. It was hot, and dresses were easy, but this wasn't quite what she had in mind when she pulled it on that morning.

"Dino—"

"How long as he been asleep?" Dino interrupted, his brow raising curiously.

"About twenty minutes."

"Good, we have time."

"I'd like to keep talking about—"

"There's nothing to talk about, Karen."

Well, she disagreed there, but it seemed like Dino wasn't going to give her much of a choice but to rest back and enjoy what he was about to do to her.

"You're trying to distract me," Karen murmured when his fingers slid under her thong.

"Is it working?"

"You tell me."

His digits swept her sex, dragging the wetness of her arousal up to her clit where he stayed for a moment, circling the nub with firm strokes. It took very little for Karen's body to start reacting to Dino's touch—it knew what it wanted, even if it was betraying her at the same damn time.

Dino smirked. "I think it is."

Asshole.

He was too smug for his own good.

Then, before she could even blink, his fingers were back down at the entrance of her pussy and thrusting in. Two fingers filled her full, while he used his thumb to put pressure down on her clit at the same time. Karen's legs widened for Dino and she couldn't help but fall right into his trap.

She liked it there, anyway.

He dropped down to his knees, his free hand bunching up the skirt of her dress and holding it high to her waist. For a little while, he simply watched his fingers fucking her under her thong before he leaned forward and then he was *all* there.

His mouth was hot against her sex—the textured plains of his tongue driving into her clit had her head falling back. His rhythm, his intent, was brutal, determined to get her off quick and harsh, whether she fought the orgasm or not.

Karen's fingers found their way into Dino's hair, holding him closer to her sex as he ate her like he was starved, and she felt her peak rising.

"Fuck, fuck, *fuck*," Karen mumbled.

Almost there ...

Dino pulled away just as her orgasm had really started to peak, and she almost wanted to kill him for stopping.

He looked up at her. "Don't watch the news for the next little while, okay?"

Karen shook her head a bit. "What?"

"You heard me."

"You had to tell me that *now*?"

Dino smiled.

Then, he went back to fucking her beautifully with his mouth until she was a shaking, panting mess against the cupboard.

She realized his intent as she came.

Of course, he had told her that *then*.

It was just more distractions.

CHAPTER 27

Dino

DINO read over the text message again as he pulled into an alleyway next to the restaurant owned by the head Capo of the Rossi family.

You wanted to know when I was bringing Lily home. We're leaving in a few.

That was it. That was all Damian Rossi's message had said.

Dino was grateful the guy had followed his orders and let him know that Lily was safely out of the restaurant. He hadn't planned for her to be inside at all, having dinner with the boss of the Outfit, their uncle Ben, and a variety of others that had been invited to dine with Terrance that day.

When he had gotten the call that Damian was invited to the dinner, and he had been asked to bring Lily along, Dino damn near refused to allow his sister to go.

Except he couldn't.

No one, not even a woman, was allowed to shun a boss.

It seriously fucked Dino's plans up, but he fixed that easily enough by demanding Damian send him a message to let him know when they would be leaving the place. Dino had been waiting for that message for an hour, just a block away from the restaurant, and now he finally had it. He'd taken his sweet time driving down the block and into an alleyway directly beside the street that would take him right by the large floor-to-ceiling windows where the Outfit people were dining.

He hadn't wanted to do this, not really.

But someone hadn't given him much of a choice.

Seems Damian *was* going to need a little push to make him follow through on his side of Dino's plans regarding the Outfit, as Dino had expected the guy would. He was all too aware that Damian was the kind of man who waited and waited, only striking when he thought it was best.

Dino didn't have time for that kind of lag.

So, what he had planned today would get shit moving in the right direction, no doubt. If not for Damian to make his moves, then for others to make theirs, which would likely force the hand of other families in the Outfit.

That was just how this shit worked.

And damn, maybe if he was lucky, Dino might get one of the three people he was gunning for today. Then, he wouldn't have to worry about doing much after that.

The families of the Outfit were predictable.

Dino had known for a long time that it wouldn't take much to make them turn on one another like they had done so many times in the past. They only needed someone to blame, or a way to climb higher in the organization, and all hell would break loose.

He fully believed that was what would happen after today.

Once the families were in the thick of fighting amongst one another; once his uncle was dead in the ground and the men who might look to him for Ben's death were also gone; once the attention was on everyone else *but* him, Dino was free to go.

He could leave.

Or that was the plan.

He still needed to fill Karen in on it, but he would … soon.

Dino pulled on his black leather riding gloves, and reached for the rapid-fire assault weapon he had sat in the passenger seat. He double-checked the safety, and then the clip just to be extra careful.

He needed this attack on the families to go off without a hitch.

He didn't have time to consider who else was sitting at the table with his uncle, the boss, and the front boss for the Outfit.

If he aimed high, he'd pepper the ceiling, break the windows, and make a scene. As much as he wanted to direct the shots right at his uncle, Dino knew he couldn't do that and safely miss everyone else sitting at the table.

He figured making a scene was enough to cause suspicion to

brew in the family.

That was always enough to cause a war.

Dino pulled his car out onto the quiet street, rolling his window down as he went and resting the rifle out the window, pointed high and ready to go. He had to do the attack fast, and he wouldn't have much time from the moment the bullets started firing to the second he would need to get the hell out of there.

His finger pulled back the trigger the moment the windows of the restaurant were in his view and he was able to see the people sitting in the private dining area.

They didn't even see him coming.

It happened so fast …

They probably didn't even see his white Bentley leave.

Dino watched the days crawl into weeks, and then a month had passed, seemingly before he even had the chance to blink and watch it go.

All the while, tensions grew in the four families that made up the Outfit. What had once seemed like such a strong foundation of people within an organization that had managed to control the city of Chicago for the better part of almost a century, had now started to crumble under the weight of suspicion and anger.

Dino had made the mistake of assuming that no one would likely be hurt the day he shot up the Rossi restaurant—he hadn't considered someone might take a bullet and die, because he couldn't afford to care at the time.

His actions took away the wife of Riley Conti, the Outfit's front boss. A bullet to her head had damn near blown off her face.

She was a mother of two.

A mother, like his had been.

Publically, Dino did what he needed to by going to Mia Conti's funeral, and expressing his condolences. He felt guilty for her grieving children, but he felt very little for her angry, agonized husband.

After all, it had been Riley who had once beaten Theo with a metal chair, nearly killing him. It was Riley who didn't think twice about turning on his boss after his wife was killed, blaming everyone in the Outfit *except* Dino, the man who actually did the shooting.

Then again, no one knew it had been him.

So, while he felt guilt over killing a woman who was—for all purposes—an innocent, her death had been to Dino's advantage. Killing her had, essentially, done what he needed for it to do. No one was looking at him, now. No one cared about Dino DeLuca, with his upcoming trial and the official attention that wouldn't wane no matter how hard he tried to deflect it.

No one cared about him at all.

He wanted to leave, to keep his promises to Karen and take them away where the judicial system of their country would never be able to touch him so that he never had to see the inside of a prison again, but he wasn't ready yet.

The job wasn't done yet.

His brother and sister weren't safe yet.

"Was it you that got Damian to do the shooting on the Conti bar?" Theo demanded.

Dino ran a hand through his hair and kept walking down the hallway. "Keep your voice down—Lily is sleeping."

That girl could sleep through a damn hurricane.

What he really wanted was for Theo to stop asking him questions.

"Dino, talk to me!"

He shouldn't be surprised that his brother had started looking to him for some of the things happening within the Outfit. Dino had needed the tensions to grow—the divide to widen—between the families over the last month. If it had seemed like, for any reason, the people might be coming together, he had purposely thrown a wrench in those plans.

Urging Damian to make his own family appear to pick a side, to irritate the Contis even more than they already were, had done just that.

"How do you even know it was Damian?" Dino asked. "Nobody knows who was in that car. It's Serena Rossi's car, Theo."

Theo snorted. "You're fucking with me, right?"

"No. I'm asking a serious question."

"Laurent and Serena drink themselves damn near to death every single night. Everybody knows it, Dino. And the only person in this organization who is even remotely good at breaking into places and stealing things without people knowing it was him is Damian. The only reason he might do this would be for *you*."

Theo was too smart for his own good.

Dino wished his brother would just leave it alone.

"Stop worrying about it, Theo," Dino demanded, turning on his brother and stopping them both in the hallway. "Stay out of it."

"Are you doing this to the Outfit, to the people?" Theo asked quietly. "Did you start this feud—*why*, Dino?"

"Would it matter if I had?"

Theo blinked, taking a step back. "What?"

"Exactly what I said, little brother. Would it matter if I was the person who had started this, who had antagonized these already-violent people into a war that they have been two steps away from starting with one another for years? Would it matter if I was the person who had a hand in pushing people along in seeing how truly awful they really are to one another?"

"Dino—"

"All these people, they turned a blind eye to Ben beating the hell out of us for years," Dino interrupted. "The boss never said a thing about all those black eyes, the broken bones we had. No one thought twice when three kids were orphaned because their mother was murdered simply because she was in the *same fucking house as their father*!"

Theo swallowed hard, taking yet another step back from his brother. "I don't want to know for sure what you do because—"

"Plausible deniability," Dino spat. "Don't worry, I've looked out for you all your fucking life, Theo. I took more hits from Ben for you than I care to count, just so he would leave you the hell alone. Chill, this isn't any different. I'm only doing what one of us won't, right?"

Theo didn't respond that time.

Dino didn't need him to.

Cherry-red Stingray.

Bumblebee-yellow Maserati.

Dino put the black suburban that he'd picked up off a guy who had wanted it to disappear, due to its involvement with a theft a few weeks earlier into drive. He'd learned his lesson the first time when after shooting up a Conti business, there had been a few people involved who were quite adamant that the car used in the drive-by shooting had been white in color.

He wasn't about to make that mistake again.

Cherry-red, bumblebee-yellow, Dino repeated silently.

Those were the vehicles belonging to his brother and sister. Those were the vehicles that would be parked, along with several others, somewhere in the Trentini driveway when Dino blew past and shot the place up.

This time, unlike the last time, Dino had targets.

Several targets.

And this time, unlike the last time, Dino had seriously considered the people who might lose their life because of his choices. But he was already knee-deep into this plan, and he couldn't back down when he was so close to the finish line that he could practically see it right in front of his face.

He'd done all of this, started a war within his own family and within an organization he had called home for years, because it had never been home to him, but rather, a prison that wouldn't let him go. A gilded cage that had promised to take away his freedom, and did little to pay him back for the loyalty and devotion he had given to it over the many years of his life.

He supposed he should care more about what he had done.

He didn't.

That was what the Outfit did to the people inside it.

It killed them slowly from the inside, and no one cared to notice.

No one cared to help.

Three homemade Molotov cocktails rested in his lap, something else to make a good show of what he was about to do. Dino's window rolled down quickly as he approached the gated entrance to the Trentini mansion, and he could see the iron gate already opening to allow the guests to yet another Outfit dinner leave the home.

People were swarming the driveway.

Dino only focused on the things he needed to make sure didn't get any bullets that might kill—cherry red, and bumblebee yellow.

It was a risk, one he probably shouldn't be willing to take, but he was going to do it anyway. He didn't bother to throw the vehicle in park as his gun was pointed out the window, but rather, stuck his foot down hard on the brake pedal to keep the Suburban from rolling ahead as he finished the final details to a plan he had never thought would work out like it had.

The trigger of the assault rifle pulled easily under the weight of his finger.

He watched bullets plow into pavement, into the stone pillars of the Trentini gate, and into the cars in the driveway. He took the shots he needed to, the ones he had planned for. Bullets flew into the back of his brother's cherry-red Stingray, and then more burrowed into the back window of Lily's bumblebee-yellow Maserati.

Damian would keep Lily safe, and Theo knew to keep down to the ground when bullets shredded the air.

Or at least, that's what Dino was hoping for.

His aim narrowed on the large white doors of the mansion and the people fleeing on the steps. Screams sliced through the air, but he wasn't focusing on those sounds. He couldn't, not if he wanted to finish this once and for all.

He let more bullets fly, recognizing the shapes of people falling on the steps, and knowing who was probably standing there.

It was always the same people who stood on those steps at the end of an Outfit gathering to say goodbye.

The boss. His family. Ben. His wife.

They liked to be above everyone else, looking down.

Dino hadn't thought this day would be any different.

"Ben made it through surgery," Theo said on the other end of the call.

Dino tried to feign interest, and failed. "Huh."

"They're putting him in a coma to give him a chance to heal without stress, but he's going to be paralyzed, and bedridden for a long time."

Dino attempted to find some sense of guilt within himself, and yet he found nothing.

It just wasn't there.

"Thanks for the heads-up," Dino said before hanging up the call.

Then, just as quickly, he called someone else.

Someone who could finish the job he thought he had done.

Damian Rossi picked up on the second ring. "Rossi speaking."

"I'm going to make it easy on you," Dino said, "and say you won't have to do very damn much except show up and pull the plugs."

"What—Dino?"

"Who else calls you from this number?"

Damian sighed. "It's … ten at night, man. I just got Lily to go to bed."

Dino managed a smile, happy his sister had finally opened up a little to her soon-to-be husband. The two were getting along much better.

"Where are you?" Damian asked. "You didn't come back to the house after—"

"I don't talk about that," Dino interrupted.

Damian had known about Dino's attack before it happened, but only because Lily had been expected to show at that stupid dinner at the mansion, and he needed her to be safe.

"I'm doing things tonight," Dino added. "Work."

Or not.

"What do you want?" Damian asked.

"Ben—I want him gone. That deal we made; your end of the bargain was to keep Lily safe at all costs, so do that, and finish the job I started."

"I heard he is—"

"Do what you need to do."

With that, Dino hung up the phone.

The fact was simple, no matter if he liked it or not.

Ben DeLuca could not be trusted, he could not be allowed to live. The power of his manipulation and control over the DeLuca siblings had been years in the making, and just because he was injured, or wheelchair-bound for the rest of his life, did not and would never undermine his ability to hurt Dino, his brother, or his sister.

Dino couldn't let that happen.

He wouldn't give Ben the chance to hurt the people he cared about one more time.

It was the last piece to his puzzle.

Once Ben was gone, then Dino could be finally be free.

He could *live*.

Dino tried to clear his mind as he pulled up to a familiar, tucked-away cabin that felt far more like home than anything else ever had. Karen had stayed there, no questions asked. She never argued with him when he said she might need to stay a while longer.

She liked it there, too.

He liked that she was safe with his son.

Dino parked his car and wasted no time making his way inside. He found his son sleeping in the upstairs loft, tucked into Karen's side with his little thumb stuck firmly in his mouth. Junior usually slept by himself, but Dino didn't mind.

He undressed down to his T-shirt and boxer-briefs, crawling into bed to be closer to his heart and soul.

He no longer held onto those things.

He'd given them to people much more worthy of them than he had ever been.

CHAPTER 28

Dino

THE wedding—one of the final things Dino was waiting for—was only days away. Maybe that was why Dino's mind was so distracted, instead of focused on the song Junior was singing that Karen had taken a whole week to teach him.

Guilt climbed up his spine with punishing steps when Junior stopped singing, glanced up at his father expectantly, and Dino couldn't even remember *what* song his son had sang.

His distraction was not missed by Karen who shot him with a curious but concerned look. He shook his head, wanting to brush off whatever concern she might be feeling, but knew at the same time, it probably wouldn't do him very much good.

She was too smart for her own good.

She knew him too well.

"Itsy Bitsy Spider," Karen mouthed.

"Thanks," he said back.

"Daddy, do you like Junior's song?" his toddler asked again.

Dino nodded, amused that his son had taken to talking about himself in the third person again. It was something he did on and off, depending on Karen's tolerance for it. Sometimes she let it slide, other times she corrected him on it. Dino went with whatever Karen was doing about it that day.

"I loved it," Dino said.

Junior smiled widely.

Always so proud.

Always so grateful.

"Here, J, go take a cookie and play in the sunroom," Karen said quietly.

Junior took the chocolate chip cookie his mother offered, and off he went without question, though he did toss a look over his shoulder to see if anyone was following him. Specifically, he looked to Dino.

Dino would follow along soon.

He had a feeling Karen wanted to talk.

He wasn't wrong.

"What's up?" Karen asked.

Dino reached for her hand, and once he had a hold of it, he tugged gently, pulling her down to his side on the couch. Closer was better—she calmed him like she always had. "Busy week, lots of things are happening next week."

"Like what?"

"My sister's wedding."

Karen's eyes grew wider. "Oh. But that's good, right?"

Dino nodded. "Sure."

"Then why do you sound like someone kicked your dog?"

"Do I?"

"Yes," Karen said, laughing softly.

"I just ..." Dino trailed off, looking back in the direction his son had gone. "I guess I just realized today that I'm almost at the end and I haven't really considered what I'm going to do when I get there."

Karen sat up a little straighter on the couch, and she avoided his gaze. "You mean the trial?"

"No."

"I thought—"

"I'm not going back to prison, Karen."

That stance of his hadn't changed, and it wasn't going to.

Not now.

Not ever.

His lawyer did his thing. His trial was scheduled to happen pretty soon, which was why he demanded Lily's wedding happen so quickly as well. But he wasn't going to make it that far—he wasn't making a home in a prison block.

"I don't ... understand," Karen said lamely.

"Morocco, Nepal, Russia, Vatican. Pick one."

Karen blinked. "Pardon?"

"Pick one, Karen. Any one of those countries—there are more, actually, but those are a few that come to mind."

"Aren't those countries that don't have extradition treaties with the United States?"

Dino nodded once. "Pick one and I'll get us there before you can even blink."

"But—"

"That's the only plan I have. Otherwise, it's trial, prison, and visitation for the next twenty or so years. Do you understand?"

"Of course. I just hadn't thought about …"

"Leaving," Dino finished for her.

"Exactly."

"But would you?" he asked quietly. "Would you leave with me when I go?"

For a long while, Karen simply stared at Dino, saying nothing. The longer she stayed silent, the more his anxiety grew. Chicago had become like a home for her, and her parents still lived across the country, waiting on her yearly visits that she'd tried to make every year since Junior was born.

He didn't want to take her away.

He didn't want to force her.

But …

"I don't want to leave you behind," Dino said, shrugging. "We've got years doing this together—trying to figure this out. You would do fine without me, I know you would, but it kills me to think about it. I wonder if you want more children someday with me; do you think you could be happy with me every day and not just a couple of days a week? I'm still trying to figure out who I am without all of this shit hanging over my shoulder. What kind of man am I, who could I have been? I want to have the chance to find out who he is."

Karen's eyes glazed with tears before the wetness dampened her lashes, and then fell, making slow tracks down her cheeks. Dino didn't reach out to wipe the moisture from her cheeks like he usually would, but only because she was due her emotions. He never wanted to take them from her.

"I know who he is," Karen said, "but I thought you had already figured that out, too."

"Not by a long shot."

Karen frowned. "Don't you already know without needing to ask me, Dino?"

"I don't know anything anymore."

"I'll go wherever with you. You only have to ask."

Because she loved him, he realized.

Karen had never cared much about the details, or the parts of him he kept tucked away. She didn't ask to see the monsters biting at his back day and night, she just cared for the man sitting beside her when he allowed her to. She didn't want to be a part of the life that suffocated him, and maybe that was what kept her so perfect away from it all. She never talked about the funerals he had gone to over the last month, but he suspected she thought he might have had a hand in at least one of them.

His uncle's, to be specific.

No, Karen didn't care.

She just loved him—loved the fuck out of him.

"Pick one," Dino repeated, "and we'll go."

Karen nodded. "Okay."

She didn't ask how or when.

He wasn't surprised.

"Hey, Dino."

Dino's head flew up from the screen of his cell phone as he walked out of the strip club. Business hours were about to start soon, and he wasn't interested in sticking around. Lily's wedding was the next day, so he needed to be up bright and early for all of that.

"Dean," Dino said, trying to beat back his urge to scowl.

Walter Artino's son leaned against the brick wall of the club looking like he owned the damn place. Except he didn't; Dino did.

He still didn't trust this kid, or the guy's snake of a father.

Ever since Ben's death, the Artinos had been making things particularly difficult for Dino and Theo on the business side of things. All too often, Dino found himself locked in a battle of wills with Walter on things like territory and splitting up crews.

Walter felt entitled, due to his friendship with Ben.

Dino felt like putting a bullet in Walter *and* Dean's head.

He couldn't afford the attention, so he chose not to do it.

Yet.

Dino looked the Artino kid up and down. "You need something?"

"Could you give me a ride home?" Dean asked.

It seemed innocent enough, but something felt off about the whole thing. Dean was more likely to ask for something from Theo, not Dino. If only because Theo had more patience for the kid and his nonsense, and he worked under Theo a great deal of the time.

It was odd for him to ask Dino for anything, really.

"To your father's place?" Dino asked.

Dean nodded.

It was on the way to Dino's home, and he didn't actually have a reason to refuse, except to be an asshole.

"Fine, but don't touch shit in my car."

Dean didn't listen to Dino's one demand.

Dino made a couple of stops—once at a corner store for gas, and another at the store closer to his house for a bottle of wine he planned to open up for Lily tomorrow morning. Each time Dino got back inside his Bentley, Dean had turned the fucking radio station off Dino's favorite one and onto some whining country station.

"If you touch my radio one more time," Dino threatened, "I'll break your fingers off and shove them down your throat."

Dean's brow flew high. "Sorry, man."

Dino had one last stop to make before he dropped Dean off, and that was to mail something off to his lawyer at the post office. The place was closed, but he'd already readied the envelope with the needed stamps, so he just shoved it in the slot, knowing the workers would mail it first thing in the morning. He wouldn't have time for it tomorrow.

Sure enough, when Dino got back in his car, Dean had turned the radio station *again*.

This time, Dino didn't threaten the kid.

But he didn't like that Dean seemed as if he was purposely

trying to piss him off, either.

He dropped Dean off at his father's without so much as a "fuck off" and headed to his own home, going twenty over the legal limit. Theo's cherry-red Stingray was parked in the driveway, freshly painted, it seemed.

He must have finally gotten his car fixed after Dino had littered it with bullets that day in the Trentini driveway, although, Theo didn't know it was his brother who had done that. He just assumed he knew things. Dino didn't confirm or deny.

Surprisingly, Theo was sitting on the front stoop, instead of inside where he usually was.

"Finally figured out what an emergency is and is not, huh?" Dino asked.

Theo shrugged. "Nice night, actually."

"Where's Lily?"

"Out with Abriella, I think."

Wonderful.

"She better not come home drunk," Dino said more to himself. "She's getting married tomorrow."

"Let her have fun."

"Yes, because *you* won't be the one dragging her from the bathroom tomorrow morning."

Theo didn't deny it. "What took you so long to get home? I know what time you left the club. I made it here before you did."

"Made a couple stops. Oh, and that fucking tool—Artino's kid—needed a drive home."

Theo frowned. "What?"

"Dean. He wanted me to drive him home."

"I asked him if he needed a drive tonight, Dino. He said no."

Dino's hand froze against the deadbolt lock just as he had started to slide the key in. "You asked him and he said no."

It wasn't even a question.

"Right before you came out. I knew you were leaving, so I was going for the night, too. Big day tomorrow. I always ask if he needs a way home, just in case. This is the first time all month he didn't go with me."

Yet, he *had* gone with Dino.

And bugged the hell out of him the whole time.

It just felt … off.

Dino wasn't one to ignore intuition.

In their life, it saved lives.

"Something is going on there," Dino said, looking to his brother.

Theo cocked a brow. "You think Dean is planning something?"

"Him, his father; what fucking difference does it make? I don't trust them."

"They don't give us a lot of reasons to," Theo admitted.

Dino decided to wave it off, if only because he had the wedding to deal with, and then a busy week after. His attention was going to focusing on his plan to get the hell out of the country with Karen as soon as humanly possible.

Theo could deal with the Artino bunch.

He was smart enough.

"Dig into that for me?" Dino asked.

Theo nodded. "Sure, man."

Dino watched the week pass by with a slowness he hadn't experienced in years. His sister's wedding had gone off without a hitch, for the most part.

Church had become a near constant in Dino's life. He could remember being a young child, and sitting beside his mother in a pew as she clutched her rosary and sang along with the hymns. Those happened to be some of his sweetest memories, and ones he shared with no one but himself, if only because they were so untainted by the realities of life.

That was probably why, when in church, Dino was the most relaxed he had ever been.

Church was his safe place—bad things didn't happen here.

Or so he thought.

"DeLuca, a word?" Tommas asked.

Dino turned to face Tommas Rossi, a cousin and close friend to Damian, his sister's new husband, less than impressed to be bothered just as he was readying to find a pew. He didn't plan on

visiting his mother's grave today, as Karen was waiting on him—
she'd asked him to come over. He promised to be there on time.
He was late earlier in the week.

Lily had also invited him for supper, but he figured he could
make that, too. He owed it to his sister, as it might be one of the
very last suppers they had together.

"What, Tommas?" Dino asked.

Tommas nodded his head to the side, directing Dino away from
the people. He followed, but his disinterest was clear. Once they
were safely away from prying eyes and ears, Tommas shoved his
hands in his pocket, a clear sign of the man's nervousness.

For the most part, Tommas was good.

A Rossi, sure, but good.

The Outfit people were still fighting. They still clawed at one
another's throats every chance they could. Dino had taken a wide
step back from it all. It seemed like, for the moment, Tommas was
another man who removed himself.

Dino could appreciate that.

"Did you know the Artinos have been cozying up to the
Trentinis lately?" Tommas asked.

Dino hadn't. "No, but I'm not concerned. They're snakes,
they're going to slither into whatever grass feels warmest to them at
the time."

Tommas nodded. "Sure, sure."

"What?"

"I just … heard some shit, thought it was odd."

"*You're* cozying up to the Trentinis, too?"

Tommas scowled, glancing to the side. "No, more like a girl
that keeps me informed."

Dino didn't need more of an explanation. "Abriella, you mean.
Terrance's granddaughter. You're still messing with her? That's
going to get you killed someday."

"Clearly, I am not good at hiding that."

"Pardon?"

"Too many people seem to know."

"As long as they keep it secret, I suppose you're good," Dino
noted.

Tommas shrugged like it didn't make a difference. "She heard
something at a dinner—the Artinos were there with Joel. You
know he's trying to head the family, now that Terrance is dead and

all."

Dino didn't blink at the mention of the boss's death.

Terrance had been killed the night of Lily's wedding.

Damian had done his damn job, after all.

"What about the dinner?" Dino asked.

"Abriella said Artino was going to make a move on the DeLucas."

"I suspected that."

"He mentioned Sunday," Tommas added.

Today.

Dino had to tell Theo, and he would, soon.

At that moment, his sister had caught his attention, coming into the church with her new husband. Late. Dino thanked Tommas, but went after Lily and Damian.

He'd deal with the Artino thing later.

Dino hit the unlock button on his key fob as he glanced back at the church where his sister and her new husband were standing close together and laughing.

The sight gave him a bit of relief that he hadn't been expecting to feel.

He'd worried a lot about Lily, worried that she wouldn't allow herself to be happy in her marriage made by men, but she had found it, nonetheless.

He didn't have to worry about her now.

Damian would care for her.

Theo was another one—Dino had done everything he could to set his brother up right in the Outfit, so Theo could make his own path, make his own name.

He'd been much better at it than Dino had ever been.

He'd wanted much more.

Dino almost felt … settled.

If that made any sense.

Somehow, his heart seemed *good.*

That was how he knew, even as he climbed inside his Bentley, started it up, and started to back it out of the parking lot, that his brother and sister would be just fine.

He could say goodbye, and not feeling as though he had left them hanging. He hadn't left business unfinished. He'd done what he promised his parents all those years ago when he buried them; he'd taken care of his siblings the best way he knew how.

All those thoughts jumbled around in Dino's mind as he reached for the tuner dial on his radio—irritated that it wasn't on his favorite station.

That was his first clue something was wrong.

Dino had already turned the knob to his station when he realized his mistake.

It was slight hiss from his dash that had him slamming back in his seat, and reaching for the door. He just got the Bentley's driver door opened when the bomb blew.

He woke up to the sounds of people screaming, to his skin *hurting,* and to the inside of the car door handle still attached to his hand.

He couldn't see the people, but he could hear them. Actually, all he could see was the stone fence that surrounded the graveyard, one that was just a little too high for people to see through.

Had he gotten thrown that far?

Had opening his door just as the pressure blew saved his life?

Dino stood, his head ringing, his ears bleeding, and his body feeling like it as going to fall apart. He couldn't catch a proper breath. He could barely hear, the longer he stood there.

But he could see the flames and the black smoke over that fence—he could hear his sister screaming his name, and the sounds of people fleeing.

No one came into the graveyard.

No one saw him.

Dino almost wondered …

Was he dead?

He was in far too much pain to be dead.

Nobody else knew it, though.

CHAPTER 29

Karen

"J, GET off the counter!"

Karen pulled the giggling, squirming toddler down, put him to the floor, and gave him the sternest look she could manage. Junior laughed in her face, and then ran off in search of something else to climb.

That kid was going to make her go gray.

"And stay out of the bathroom!" Karen shouted after her son.

Junior didn't respond, but that wasn't unusual. His new favorite way to find trouble included seeing what exactly he could make disappear down the toilet. Thankfully, he hadn't clogged it yet.

Hoping her son wasn't looking for trouble, and had decided to play in his back bedroom, Karen went to work in the kitchen. She wanted to have lunch with Dino, but if she didn't start cooking something now, it wouldn't be done by the time he got there from the church.

Absently, to fill the silence, she turned on the small flat screen TV in the kitchen while she worked. A random news channel with several anchors sitting around a curved table doing some sort of panel on the latest economy numbers.

She didn't care to hear them talk, so she turned it on low, just enough for their murmurs to keep her from worrying too much about what Junior might be doing.

Dino had told her to stop hovering so much over the boy, and to let him explore. He was a smart child, maybe too smart for his own good, and he needed to expel his energy or he was going to expel it in worse ways.

Karen decided to give it a try.

Dino had been willing to clean the messes, after all.

She got so lost in chopping vegetables that she barely caught the flyby of her son as he ran past her, giggling about something. Turning to watch him run up the spiral staircase that led to the upper loft, something on the television screen caught her attention.

It'd only been a few minutes, she thought.

The panel should have still been on there talking.

Except ... they weren't.

A whole new picture was beginning to take shape on the screen. Smoke hanging heavily in the sky, charred ground, frightened, crying people, and a twisted mess of a vehicle that was burned right down to the fucking ground.

Karen stilled in place, watching the scene unfold.

The woman on the television was talking, explaining what had happened, her voice a quiet murmur in the cabin's large kitchen. Perhaps she should have turned the television up, listening to the *Breaking News* unfolding in the heart of Chicago, but she couldn't bring herself to do it.

Why?

She recognized that parking lot. She recognized the church behind it and the large stone wall surrounding a cemetery where she had once photographed a beautifully lonely man cleaning the headstone belonging to his mother.

It didn't matter, Karen came to realize slowly.

She didn't have to turn up the volume at all. The headline rolled across the bottom of the screen, explaining the details for those who might just be passing a television by and didn't want to stop long enough to listen to the broadcast.

Breaking News, it read. *Bombing. One suspected dead. Victim identified as Dino DeLuca ...*

Karen stopped reading. She didn't need to know what he was affiliated to, his age, or that his siblings had been in the parking lot, too. She already knew those things.

She knew everything about him.

Karen had been wrong.

Once, she had thought to herself, if she had to, she could live without Dino. It would hurt, her soul would be gone, leaving a black, empty space full of pain and loneliness, but she could do it if she needed to.

She could live without her soul, she had said.

She had been so terribly wrong.

Karen only realized how wrong she had been when her knees hit the hardwood floor of the kitchen, tears spilling as she screamed for no other reason than to give her sudden shock of pain a way to escape from her body.

And she thought … *this is what dying inside feels like.*

She had been wrong.

There was no such thing as life without a soul.

Black mood.

Black heart.

Black day.

Black dress.

Karen thought it was all appropriate that her mood, the way she felt, the day, and her dress all managed to match the color of mourning for the day of Dino's funeral. If anything, it would allow her to blend in with the rest of the mourners, and she wouldn't draw attention with her presence.

Or at least, that was her hope.

She had to say goodbye.

She deserved to say goodbye.

Karen had waffled on the idea of bringing Junior, too, if only because this funeral was for his father, and while he was too young to understand Dino was dead, he was not too young to understand that his daddy hadn't been around for more than two weeks.

He asked for his father every day. He held up the last T-shirt Dino had given him, wanting a new one. He woke up every morning and searched for his father. He broke Karen's heart with each crestfallen expression, when he realized Dino was still not there like he needed and wanted him to be.

Somehow, Karen had managed to talk herself out of bringing Junior to the funeral. It hadn't been an easy choice, but she knew it was the smarter one, as far as that went. There would likely be pictures of Dino for the mourners to look over before they took their seats and the funeral began, as was customary for most ceremonies.

Karen thought if Junior saw a picture he recognized, he might have a fit, or even just point out to anyone who would listen that the man in the picture was his dad.

They weren't a part of these people's lives.

They weren't a part of this at all.

That was what Dino had always told Karen. He'd kept them away and safe from it all.

She intended to do the same.

Karen took a back pew the very second she entered the church, sitting beside an older gentleman with a hat on the top of his head that made him look like he had come straight out of the dirty thirties. She found the people she believed to be Dino's family— his siblings—in the very front row, accepting hugs, handshakes, and quiet apologies.

She recognized Theo, but not the blonde woman at his side.

Lily, maybe.

Dino's sister.

The slight glimpse she got of the woman's profile confirmed what she thought—those DeLuca genes were strong, and Lily shared both her brothers' features, although a prettier, feminine version.

The young woman's pain was as clear as day, and it only amplified the ache starting to grow in the middle of Karen's chest.

She'd ignored it for so long.

She did what she needed to in order to keep moving for her son.

And yet here ... now ... she found herself leaning forward, her hand grasping the curved edge of the back of the pew in front of her, as a sob rose in her chest and caught painfully in her throat.

She couldn't do this.

She shouldn't be here.

That casket at the front—closed and gleaming—caught her eye.

What was left of her heart shattered, while the rest of her just felt so fucking numb.

"Are you okay, Miss?" the man with the hat asked Karen.

She didn't answer, simply pushed out of the pew and made a beeline for the doors of the church. She needed to get the hell out of there as fast as she possibly could.

She had just made it to the front step, one that was now empty as the people had all gathered inside on the dreary day, when a voice from behind stopped her.

"Karen, wait."

Theo.

Karen's heart hurt a little more, but she didn't stop moving forward. She kept walking, taking the church steps two at a time, ignoring the smack of shoes hitting the pavement behind her. She'd just grabbed the driver's door of her car when Theo caught up to her.

"Karen!"

"I just want to leave," she said in a mumble, fumbling with the key fob and the unlock button. "I want to get the fuck out of here."

Theo cleared his throat, shoving his hands in his pockets as he watched her warily. He never came any closer, and Karen appreciated that. She was not in the mood for comfort of any sort.

"I need to go pick up J from the daycare and get the hell out of this city," Karen said, her words catching on the ache in her throat.

"How's he doing?" Theo asked.

Karen looked over at him, not sure what to say. "He's …"

"Yeah?"

"Lost."

A lot like she was.

A lot like Theo looked to be right then.

Theo shifted on his feet, glancing over his shoulder back at the church. "Listen, if you need anything, Karen … or if the baby needs something, you know where to find me."

"You can't give me what I need, Theo."

He nodded. "Yeah, I know."

"I don't even understand what happened. One day, everything was fine, and then the next, he was gone. He didn't even say anything about something like this."

"He didn't know. Nobody did. It looked like a timer bomb on his radio, so when he switched stations, it set the relay to count down three seconds before it blew up. The car burned out, but a lot of pieces were sent flying, and that was how they found part of the electronics for the bomb."

Karen wished that information helped her somehow.

Just knowing *how* it all happened.

"Who?" she asked.

Theo shrugged. "I don't know, but I'm working on that. Could I, uh …"

Karen finally got that damned car unlocked, and she pulled opened the driver's door. "What, Theo?"

"Could I call you? Maybe we can meet up once a week or something."

She looked to the church. "I don't know if that's a good idea. He didn't want us around those—"

"Just me," Theo interrupted quickly. "I owe it to him—who else is going to help you with that baby, now?"

Karen nodded. "I know how to contact you."

With that, Theo said his goodbye, and Karen watched as he made his way back to the church, and then disappeared inside. A part of her wanted to go with him, to finish what she had started with Dino, and put him to rest like they both deserved.

A bigger part wouldn't allow her to let go at all.

A part that still didn't want to admit he was gone.

Karen climbed into her car, needing to get away from those thoughts. She was just starting to back out of the parking space when she had a thought …

His mother's grave.

Who would clean it now?

Who would say hello to her every Sunday like he had done for years?

Karen threw her car back in park, left her purse and everything else sitting on the passenger seat, and even the keys remained in the ignition as she got out and headed for the cemetery. She went through the large gates, the only opening in the high stone wall that kept the graves protected.

It was as empty as it always was.

She weaved in and out of tombstones, careful not to step on graves, as she found the familiar one that had started it all.

How appropriate, she thought.

How appropriate that it was here where she said goodbye.

Karen wiped the blades of grass and other dirt from the stone of Valerie DeLuca, fixing the string of rosary beads hugging the headstone. She didn't stay long, maybe only a minute or two, but she felt better when she finally stood to leave.

Not okay, not whole, but better.

It was something.

Karen turned to leave, settling herself with the idea of coming back next week to do the same, and froze right where she stood.

He sat there on that bench where she had waited for him once.

He sat there with a sad smile and brown eyes trained on her.

He sat there like a statue, cold and unmoving.

Karen wondered if she was going crazy.

God knew she had felt insane for a while, now.

Dino patted the spot beside him on the bench, never once looking away from Karen. "Come and sit. I think I have to apologize again."

Karen blinked. "You're not real. You're dead."

He couldn't be.

Dino smiled, his hand lifting to show a bandage covering a great portion of his limb. "Dead people don't feel pain, Karen."

"I'm going crazy—that's what this is."

"Would that be easier?" he asked.

Maybe.

"No," Karen settled on saying.

"Let me apologize again, Karen."

Her heart, and the soul she thought was gone forever, wouldn't let her refuse.

Even if she was crazy.

EPILOGUE

Five months later ...

Dino

THREE broken ribs.

Burns up his left hand, arm, and down his back.

Dislocated right shoulder.

Two broken toes.

A nasty gash under his jawline.

Two black eyes.

Busted blood vessels in his eyes and nose.

Internal bruising.

A concussion.

But he was alive.

Dino was alive.

He vaguely remembered the minutes after the bomb had blown, and he'd woken up in the graveyard, on the other side of the high stone fence. He'd stumbled away from the smoke and fire filling up the sky on the other side of the fence, confusion muddling his thoughts and his brain functions. He'd fallen again and again, his ears ringing, his vomit spilling to the grass as he fought to stay awake long enough to make it to the other side of the graveyard.

It'd been a long walk.

The longest fucking walk of his life.

Some driver passing by when he'd exited the other side of the graveyard had picked him up, and taken him to a nearby walk-in clinic. He'd passed out—they labeled him a John Doe, and no one came to claim him.

Lucky, he supposed.

Dino pretended like he didn't know who he was when the doctors and nurses asked, and one day, when he heard them mention that an officer would be in to question him, he snuck out of his room, and left the hospital without another look back.

Funny, he thought.

All those injuries.

The burns, the pain, the nightmares …

He had survived worse. Ben had put him through far worse, which he kept telling Karen each and every time he woke up from another dream about the bomb, and yet it hadn't *killed* him.

It should have.

He should have been dead, burned to a fucking crisp like everyone thought he had been, and buried beside his parents' graves.

Yet, he wasn't.

A fucking *bomb* hadn't killed him.

But a few stray bullets damn near killed his brother.

Dino stared across the hospital parking lot, watching as his brother stood from a wheelchair, helped by Lily on his one side and Evelina Conti on his other. He stayed hidden in his car, the dark windows keeping him from being seen, as the scene played out at the hospital entrance. It killed him inside to see his brother struggle—to see the pain flicker in Theo's face as he picked up a bag, and then gave Evelina a quick kiss on her cheek.

That—his brother's relationship—was not something Dino expected.

It wasn't a bad thing, though.

Lily fretted, moving all around Theo, her lips moving fast as they walked toward a waiting car. Their little sister was doing better, she'd accepted their life, she was moving forward. Dino couldn't ask for more, and the small swell of her stomach made him smile, though his heart broke a little at the knowledge he probably wouldn't ever get to meet her first child.

After all, if he wanted to be free, going back was not an option.

Their life had always been a prison to him.

They were doing just fine, now. Without him, they'd learned how to take care of themselves, how to make shit work, and how to survive. Theo had gone after each and every monster that Dino had left behind, and put them in a grave one by one until none were left to haunt the DeLuca siblings still living with their demons.

They had grieved.

They had smiled a little less for a while.

But they came out just fine in the end.

Dino was going to keep letting them be fine.

They didn't need him now.

He'd done his job.

He'd kept his promises.

"How did Theo look?" Karen asked as Dino entered the cabin's kitchen.

He wasn't even surprised that she knew where he had gone. It was becoming a habit for him lately. Even though he knew it was dangerous, and a little bit stupid, he found himself going into the city at least once a week to check on his brother or sister.

Up until the shooting that had nearly killed Theo, Karen too had gone out once a week to take Junior to meet up with his uncle.

Dino stayed hidden at the cabin, then. Theo never came to the cabin.

"In pain," Dino finally said.

He came up behind her, kissing the back of her neck as she washed vegetables for supper.

"And Lily?"

"Worried, and pregnant."

Karen nodded. "Theo mentioned something about that the last time we talked."

She didn't tell him a lot of details about her conversations with Theo. It was easier on Dino that way, and he could pretend like he didn't want to know because then he was allowing his siblings a real chance at life and freedom without him.

He wanted the same—they all deserved it.

"Theo called before you even got back here," Karen admitted.

Dino stiffened. "Oh?"

"Thanked me again for coming so late to visit with him and Lily that night at the hospital. He wants to see Junior when he's feeling more up to moving around."

"Sure."

"Someday, I'm going to have to start telling him no, Dino."

He knew that.

He also knew Theo probably wouldn't understand why Karen refused to take their son out to visit his uncle in the city, but like the good man he was, Theo would accept her choices.

"It's just that Junior talks about you when Theo's there, saying his daddy told him this or that, or he did this or that with his daddy," Karen said quietly. "Theo usually takes it as Junior means *before*, but as he gets older, J should understand the difference between now and then, Dino. Theo's not stupid."

"I know," Dino murmured.

"He loves that boy."

"He still will."

Karen nodded. "You hungry?"

"Starved."

"Junior wanted to go out on the boat, too."

Dino smiled. "I can do that."

Karen turned around, her gaze lit up with happiness as she stared at him. Her fingers ghosted over a couple of new scars on his cheek, some scrapes that had taken longer to heal and left nasty marks behind.

He owned a whole bunch of new marks now.

He figured they were worth it for moments like these.

Moments with Karen.

Moments with his son.

He had forever to have these moments now.

"You okay?" Karen asked.

Dino leaned down and kissed her again. "Perfect."

"Love you, Dino."

"Always, sweetheart."

He didn't exist anymore.

Not to the outside world.

Dino DeLuca was dead and buried, as far as anyone

understood. He was finally able to be the man that Karen deserved, and the full-time father he'd prayed to be for his son.

It was all he had wanted.

Yet, freedom was never quite free.

He still had to give up a lot, but he did it.

For the majority of his life, Dino had been treated as something that was worthless. A piece of waste to throw out with the trash. He certainly learned exactly what his worth was by the end of it all—he learned even waste had worth, and he hoped the people he had left behind understood it, too.

Dino regretted nothing.

ABOUT THE AUTHOR

Bethany-Kris is a Canadian author, lover of much, and mother to three very young sons, one cat, and two dogs. A small town in Eastern Canada where she was born and raised is where she has always called home. With her boys under her feet, a snuggling cat, barking dogs, and a spouse calling over his shoulder, she is nearly always writing something ... when she can find the time.

Find Bethany-Kris at:
Her website www.bethanykris.com,
or on Facebook at www.facebook.com/bethanykriswrites,
on her blog at www.bethanykris.com/blog,
or on Twitter - @BethanyKris.

Sign up to Bethany-Kris's New Release Newsletter here:
http://eepurl.com/bf9lzD.

THANK YOU!

I was so convinced for a very long time that I would not be telling Dino DeLuca's story, because well … we all knew how he ended, didn't we? And yet, at the same time, I never actively made an effort in the *War* series to write an official page of his death, something that would say for sure, no question, he was gone. I even left bits to use, things to go back and give the reader some spark of hope that maybe—maybe, maybe, maybe—he was alive, like the pictures sent to Theo, or the fact it was a closed coffin, with Theo never discussing the body of his brother that had never actually been found.

And I suppose now, we all know why it wasn't found, right?

So many readers wanted this story, even if it ended badly, even if they thought they knew how it ended for Dino, they wanted it. And I have to give them my heartfelt, most genuine thanks first, because you all were the reason I decided to sit down and create the ending Dino deserved. After all his life's worth, all he sacrificed, he certainly deserved his own private happiness that no one but him could touch. So thank you.

To my editor, Nina, thank you for being wonderful, and for pushing me to be a better writer. I am so grateful to have found you in the midst of many others. I'm not quite sure my books would come out the same way they do without your stamp of approval on them.

To my proofreaders and prereaders, Eli and Mia, thank you for jumping headfirst into the Duet, not knowing where it was leading us to, or what was going to happen, but still being so excited from the moment you read the first page. Every author needs people like you in their corner. I'm proud to have you in mine.

And to my family, all my love, thanks, and my heart. For the heart is where your home is, and mine is always with you.

—Kris

OTHER BOOKS

Filthy Marcellos

Antony
Lucian
Giovanni
Dante
Legacy
The Complete Collection

Donati Bloodlines

Thin Lies
Thin Lines
Thin Lives

The Chicago War

Deathless & Divided
Reckless & Ruined
Scarless & Sacred
Breathless & Bloodstained

The Russian Guns

The Arrangement
The Life

The Score
Demyan & Ana
Shattered
The Jersey Vignettes

Find more on Bethany-Kris's website at www.bethanykris.com.